Thomas C. Baring

Pindar in English Rhyme

being an attempt to render the Epinikian odes, with the principal remaining

fragments, into English rhymed verse

Thomas C. Baring

Pindar in English Rhyme
being an attempt to render the Epinikian odes, with the principal remaining fragments, into English rhymed verse

ISBN/EAN: 9783337262556

Printed in Europe, USA, Canada, Australia, Japan

Cover: Foto ©Andreas Hilbeck / pixelio.de

More available books at **www.hansebooks.com**

PINDAR IN ENGLISH RHYME;

BEING AN ATTEMPT TO RENDER THE

EPINIKIAN ODES,

WITH THE PRINCIPAL REMAINING FRAGMENTS, OF

PINDAR,

INTO ENGLISH RHYMED VERSE,

BY

THOMAS CHARLES BARING, M.A., M.P.,
LATE FELLOW OF BRASENOSE COLLEGE, OXFORD.

CONTENTS.

—·—

OLYMPIAN ODES.

PYTHIAN ODES.

ISTHMIAN ODES.

NEMEAN AND OTHER ODES.

FRAGMENTS.

OLYMPIAN ODES.

1. To Hiero of Syracuse.

WATER is best; and gold, as blazing fire
    Gleams far across the night,
  All pride-begetting wealth beside
    Excels in might.
But if, my own sweet soul, thou hast desire
    The games to hymn,
    'Mid all the pride
  Of heaven, throughout the desert air
Seek not to spy a star that may compare
With warming Sun himself, whom daylight cannot dim.
    Nor shalt thou know
    To celebrate in song
  A fairer strife than that Olympia shows;
    Whence, chanted to and fro,
  Through poets' skill the famous anthem flows
  In praise of Kronos' son, from those who throng
To crowd the gladsome hearth of wealthy Hiero:

A

Who culling every virtue's topmost flower
    A righteous sceptre wields
    O'er Sicily's rich apple-yards
      And harvest-fields,
Yet loves with music's gems in leisure hour
      His heart to cheer ;
    When tuneful bards,
Assembled round his friendly board,
Upraise a merry strain with one accord.
Then from its solemn peg release, and bring me here
      The Doric lyre,
    If aught in Pisa's fame,
Or Pherenikus' splendid victory,
    Had potence to inspire
The mind with sweetest thought, when easily
By dark Alpheius conquering he came
Unspurred, that great renown his master might acquire,

    The charger-loving king of Syracuse.
      His glory glows
Through all the thickly-peopled colony
Of Lydian Pelops, whom there chanced to choose
Strong earth-encompassing Poseidon's love :
    When safe the caldron pure above,

One shining shoulder shaped of ivory,
    In Klotho's arms he rose.
  For many wondrous haps have been ;
    And oft a cozening tale
  With dainty falsehoods tricked, I ween,
  Man's loud assent to win is seen,
    And sober truth to fail.

And Grace, for man who fashions all things fair
    And every pleasure gives,
  Not seldom that the false may seem
      The true contrives,
Conferring credence ; wiser witness bear
      The after days ;
    And meet, I deem,
  It is in sooth that mortal man
Should say about the gods what good he can ;
So shall his blame be less, and greater so his praise.
    Illustrious seed
    Of Tantalus, there shall
A counter-story now by me be told ;
  How when thy sire decreed
On Sipylus the stately feast to hold,
And bade th' immortals grace his festival,

Then far on high in car of gold with golden steed

The monarch who the gleaming trident sways,
Subdued by mad desire,
Upbore thee towards the blest abode,
Where dwells the Sire
Of gods, far honoured ; where in later days
Young Ganymede
Triumphant rode
To pleasure Zeus : and when they sought
And found thee not, nor home the truant brought,
To vex thy mother's ear a melancholy rede
In whispers dim
Her neighbours, jealous fools,
Related ; how when freely flowed the wine,
As o'er the flesh-pot's brim
The boiling water seethed, the guests divine
Threw in thy mangled form, and then, like ghouls,
Distributing devoured thee, severed limb from limb.

I cannot gods immortal gluttons deem.
Avaunt the thought !
For loss is aye the scandal-monger's gain.
But if Olympus' lords with high esteem

E'er honoured mortal man, then Tantalus
    Was he : but, o'er-elated thus,
He could not brook such bliss, nor could restrain
    O'erweening pride that wrought
    His bane. His insolence to pall
      His father o'er his head
    A mighty boulder hung, whose fall
    He ever seeks to fend, and all
      His merriment is fled.

And now a dreary, helpless life he leads
    Of never-ending grief,
  With comrades three the fourth sad soul
      Because, a thief,
Th' ambrosia which undying beings feeds,
    The nectar which
      They drink, he stole
    And gave to fellow-quaffers food
Which had himself with deathlessness endued.
If man have hope that crime of his can 'scape the reach
    Of God on high,
    He errs. His son therefore
The deathless from their presence drove again
    As in the days gone-by

To mingle with the short-lived race of men.
There soon as on his blackened chin he wore
A goodly growth of beard, and dreams of marriage-tie

Within him stirred his heart, he studied from
    Her Pisan father's side
    Hippodameia fair of fame
      To win for bride.
So to the margin of the gray sea-foam
    At deep of night
    Alone he came,
And hailed the thund'rous Trident-king—
Who hearing to his feet sped hurrying—
And spake : " Poseidon, if the thought of love's delight
    In former days
    Some little grace obtain,
Oinomaüs' brazen javelin paralyse ;
    On swiftest car convey
Myself to Elis ; bid my might arise ;
For suitors three and ten are with the slain,
And still his daughter's wedding rites her sire would stay.

High deeds of peril cowards cannot charm ;
    But since we all

Must die, why should man nurse inglorious age,

In darkness sitting filled with vain alarm

Without a share in all that renders life

    A pleasure?   In the coming strife,—

Do thou give happy issue,—I engage."

      He ceased.   Nor did he call

      With words of no avail.   His kind

        Intent the god to prove

      Produced a chariot golden-lined,

      And tireless horses swift as wind

        With wings to aid above.

And thus he beat Oinomaüs in the race ;

      And thus the maid he won ;

    And children six she bore her lord,

      And each a son,

A chieftain each endowed with every grace :

      And now beside

      Alpheius' ford

In pilgrim-haunted grave he lies,

Where blood-libations crown his obsequies

Hard by the stranger-crowded altar.   Far and wide

      The honour shines

      In Pelops' circus got

At green Olympia, where for rivalry
  Each festival combines
The swift of foot with those whose labours lie
In feats of strength; and he to whose glad lot
The wreath has fallen may live in peace and pleasant lines.

To-day's success is deemed his highest bliss
  By mortal man alway:
 And with Aiolia's knightly song
   'Tis mine to-day
To crown the victor whose this triumph is.
   And sure am I
   Not one among
The sons of men is living at this hour
Of fairer knowledge or of kinglier power
For bard with music's ceaseless change to glorify.
   The deity
  Who o'er the games presides,
And makes their guardianship his special care,
  Has special care of thee,
 King Hiero, and all the daily wear
Of thy pursuits: and if his love abides
A little while, I hope in sweeter minstrelsy

My pathway strewing with assistant words,
  Nigh Kronos' height
Sunlit, to laud thee for the four-horse race.
For me the Muse within her quiver hoards
A mightier arrow. Others other ways
  Excel ; but aye the crown of praise
Is borne away by kings as first in place.
  No further strain thy sight.
  Long be it thine the steeps to tread
   Of honours won in peace ;
  While thy reflected glories shed
  Distinction on thy poet's head
   Through all the realms of Greece !

2. To Theron of Akragas.

Say, sovereign of the lyre,
 Sweet Spirit of song,
What god, what man, what hero shall we sing
 With loud acclaim?
 In Pisa Zeus is king.
And fair Olympia's games by Herakles,
 The first-fruits of his war,
Were stablish'd. Theron too in victor car,
 By four fleet horses borne along,
Demands applause, who ne'er did stranger wrong,
The prop in whose support his Akragas has ease,
The prime restorer of the glorious name
 Of many a noble sire.

 Who after years of woe
  And weariness
Set up their homes and gods yon stream anigh.

And there became
Sikelia's very eye ;
When wealth and favour native worth pursued
In Fate's unswerving hand.
O Kronian son of Rhea, whose command
The prize of emulations stress,
Olympus' seat, Alpheius' passages
Obey, by these our hymns be softened, look for good
On him and his, and let their lands the same
To children's children go

For ever.   What is past and gone,
For right or wrong.
Not even Time, the matchless one,
The sire of all, can make undone ;
But yet there still may be,
With dawning of a brighter lot,
A calm forgetfulness of what
Was ill ere long.
And e'en inveterate misery
Will faint and die beneath the might
Of sweet delight ;

When on the whirling wheel
Of heavenly fate

Good luck comes uppermost.   With this agree
    The stories told
    Of Kadmus' progeny,
Who suffered evils great, till greater bliss
    Drove all their griefs away.
For 'mongst Olympus' denizens to-day
    Lives long-haired Semele in state
Whom loud-tongued levin slew, but not in hate :
Beloved of Pallas, more beloved of Zeus she is ;
    And Dionyse his ivy-branch in hold
        Is full of loving zeal.

    Fair-thronèd Ino too,
        The legends say,
    With Nereus' ocean-maidens in the sea
        Immortal dwells
        For all eternity.
To dying men it is not given to know
        The issues after death :
Nor know we surely whilst on earth beneath
        If ever 'twill be ours a day
Of quietude to close, whose sun-born ray
Unflagging pleasure cheers.   This way the currents flow
And that, and now the tide of joyance swells,

And now the tide of woe.

And thus it happed that Destiny,
  Who wont to nurse
The fortunes of this family
With heaven-conferred prosperity,
  In later times began
To blend an aye-recurring bane,
Since Laïus met his son again,
  Who bore the curse
And killed his sire, and thus the ban
Fulfilled, pronounced by lips divine
  From Pytho's shrine.

Keen-eyed Erinnys saw
  With eagle sight,
And with reciprocating homicide
  His race destroyed.
When Polyneikes died
Thersander only lived to gain renown,
  In boyish feats of strength
A conqueror at first, and then at length
  On fields where warriors lose and win
A helpful scion for Adrastus' kin.

Ainesidemus' son, thus ancestor'd, to crown
   'Tis fit the best of lyres should be employed
     And praises free of flaw.

    Himself alone he gained
      Olympia's prize :
But on the Pythian and the Isthmian field,
     Where round the course
    A dozen times are wheeled
The four-horsed cars, the Graces who dispense
    Their even favours gave
The wreaths to his twin brother, which to have
   Th' aspirant's load of care unties.
The wealth that virtue's garment beautifies,
Will opportunity provide and competence
   For this and that, by nature's deep-set force
    Of heedfulness sustained ;

    A star of far refulgent rays
     And trusty beam,
  So the possessor rule his ways,
  As conscious of the coming days ;
    How lawless souls that sin
  At once are punished dying here:

For crimes that stain this earthly sphere,
　　Where Zeus supreme
Is sovereign, judged the earth within
By one whose sentence is decreed
　　Of ruthless Need.

　　For aye, alike in gloom
　　And broad day-light,
Having a sun, a life of lesser toil.
　　The good behold :
　　Who worry not the soil
With tireless strength of hand, nor vex the sea
　　For empty livelihood.
But with the gods with awful honours dued
　　They who while living took delight
In every solemn vow performed aright,
Abide, a tearless race for all eternity.
While others suffer, sinners over-bold,
　　A sight-surpassing doom.

　　And those who have the strength
　　The ordeal thrice
In either world to bide, and keep their soul
　　From every taint

Of evil-doing whole,
The path of Zeus are privileged to tread
To Kronos' castled piles :—
Where ocean breezes round the happy isles
Blow softly ; where with sunny dyes
Blossoms of gold are blazing ; some arise
From earth on gorgeous stems, and some are water-fed,
To bind the brow and arms of each new saint
With glory's wreath at length :—

By Rhadamanthus' judgment tried
Who sits in state
To help at father Kronos' side,
Who wedded erst a queenlier bride
To fill the highest throne
Of heaven, Rhea ; 'mongst the blest
Where Peleus and where Kadmus rest,
And where elate
His mother, whose beseeching tone
The heart of Zeus to ruth had wrought,
Achilles brought,

Who Hektor overthrew,
The sole support,

The one resistless, stedfast, prop of Troy;
And Kyknus strong,
And Eos' Aithiop boy,
In combat put to death.   In wingèd rows
The arrows lie beneath
My elbow, waiting in the quiver-sheath
The fitting time to make report
To knowing folk; for those of common sort
They need interpreters.   The wise by instinct know:
The learned are a silly chattering throng,
That raven-like pursue

The bird divine of Zeus
With fruitless cry.
Arise, my soul, and bend thy bow for aim.
Whom shall we strike,
Loosing the shafts of fame
From thoughts of kind intention?—Akragas.
And loud will I proclaim,—
And call the gods to testify the same,—
With tongue that never stooped to lie,
That never town in all a century
Has brought unto the birth a citizen that was
In heart pervading kindliness the like,

B

Or bounteous hand profuse,

Of Theron.   But satiety
   To praise succeeds ;
Yet dares not be an enemy
With justice in its company,
   But underhand will go
To use the tongues of crazy men
And gossip false, to hide from ken
   Good men's good deeds.
For as the sands are countless, so
His acts of kindness manifold
   May ne'er be told.

3. To Theron of Akragas.

To please the stranger-loving sons of Tyndareus,
  And Helen famous for her tresses fair,
    By splendid Akragas's praise
For Theron's newly-won Olympic victory
      My hymn I fain would raise,
    The prize of horses' feet that tireless be.
And bent on this intent but now I saw the Muse
  Beside me, as I strove to find an air
      To fit to Doric shoes,

And brighter make the feast. The wreaths that now are tied
  Amidst his locks upon the bard impose
    This need of origin divine,
With citterns many-tongued and oboe's shriller cry
      To fittingly combine
  Full rhythmic phrases, so to magnify
Ainesidemus' son ; and Pisa magnified

Would fain be, whence the sacred hymnal flows,
    Wherever men abide,

For him, for whom, fulfilling Herakles'
    Behests of old, the judge of Greece,
      Aitolia's faultless son,
Above his brows upon his tresses lays '
The decoration twined of th' olive's branches gray ;
    Which in primeval days
    The step-son of Amphitryon
From Istros' shady sources bore away.
Fairest memorial of Olympia's victories.

With softly winning speech he begged and honest brow
    Of them that dwell the northern wind behind,
    And Phoibos' favour supplicate,
A slip that after should become a shady grove,
    Where Zeus in woodland state
Receives the homage of the world, and prove
The common crown of manly worth.   For duly now
    His father's fane had hallowed been, and kind
    The mid-month moon aglow

On car of gold her orb lit full 'gainst Evening's end ;

When on Alpheius' sacred banks he sate
   To hold the lists in equity;
Where each fifth year for strife the mighty stand arrayed :
    Yet not one lovely tree
  Throve on the soil in Kronian Pelops' glade.
So when he saw the sun's most burning rays descend
  Full on his close of verdure desolate,
    His spirit bade him wend

  To Istros' borders, where in days gone by
   Leto's fair daughter, apt to ply
    The lash and haste the steed,
  Received him, coming from the mountain-lands
And tortuous ravines of Arcady, compelled
    Eurystheus' hard commands
   By Zeus his sire and Fate to heed,
  And fetch the golden-antlered hind, of old
By Atlas' maid inscribed " Orthosia's hind am I."

So pressing on her track he saw that land of rest
  Beyond the blasts of chilly Boreas,
    And there the olive tree that grows
Therein, and stood entranced, until within his soul
    A sweet desire arose,

Where four times thrice the racing chariots roll
Around the course, to plant it.   Now a gracious guest,
　　With deep-girt Leda's godlike twins, he has
　　　　Vouchsafed at our request

To grace the present feast.   For when he parted hence
　　For courts Olympian, them he bade preside
　　　　O'er all the wondrous rivalry
Of manly excellence and cars at top of speed.
　　　　So to th' Emmenidæ,
　　And Theron here, my soul proclaims the meed
Is due, which Tyndareus' well-mounted sons dispense :
　　For they of men the guestive boards provide
　　　　At lavishest expense,

With pious heart the holy mysteries
　　Preserving.   And as water is
　　　　The best of all, and gold
All other gains excels ; so Theron's power
And long-descended worth have reached their zenith, heard
　　　　Where high the pillars tower
　　　　That Herakles set up of old.
　　Beyond nor foolish man nor wise has steered.
Nor mine be now the task : 'twere wasted work, I wis !

4. To Psaumis of Kamarina.

HAIL Zeus supreme, untiring thunder's charioteer !
  For thine alone
The circling seasons are, which bring me here
  The mightiest of strifes to see,
  And list the ever-changing tone
   Of cittern's voice.
When friends succeed the tale of their success
   To hear the good rejoice.
  Then hear me, Son of Kronos, king
Of Etna's mount, whose breezy heights oppress
Enormous Typhon's hundred-headed might ;
   And of thy kindliness,
   The Graces to delight,
   Accept the masque we bring
To celebrate Olympia's newest victory,

The everlasting light of stalwart thews renown :
      Which comes for sake
Of Psaumis' team, who, wreathed with olive crown
    In Pisa won, is hot with haste
  For Kamarina fame to make.
        May heaven befriend
The prayers he yet may utter.   Praise from me
       Shall evermore attend
   One who is bent the horse to train,
And joys in boundless hospitality,
And strives his best with purity of soul
      In safe tranquillity
      His city to control.
     My words I will not stain
With falsehood. Trial shows the worth of man at last.

     By proven prowess thus
     The son of Klymenus
From Lemnian women's jeers was freed, when he
The foot-race won in brazen arms arrayed :
   And as he went to claim his crown
    From queen Hypsipyle,
     " Fair lady," said,
" Behold ! how swift I am of foot is shown :

Nor weaker are my hands, nor slower beats my heart :
     Yet oft to youthful brow
     The freaks of Fate impart,
Contrasting manhood's prime, untimely locks of snow."

5. To Psaumis of Kamarina.

THE sweetest, fairest, crown
Olympia's games can give,
To guerdon mightiest renown,
With gladsome heart receive,
Daughter of Ocean, looking down
On Psaumis and his wagon here,
Psaumis, who brings his gifts, th' untiring muleteer :

Who fain to aggrandize
The city named for thee
Has caused the six twin altars rise,
To bounteous feast and free
Bidding th' immortals from the skies
By oxen slain with priestly knife,
And five protracted days of agonistic strife.

He drove his steeds and mules; alone he rode :
    And, Kamarina, still to thee
    The gentle fame his prowess owed
He gave, proclaiming with his victory
His father Akron's name, and newly built abode.

    Protecting Pallas, see,
    From that beloved shore,
    Where Pelops and Oinomaüs be
    At rest for evermore,
He comes to hymn the purity
Of yonder grove thy shrine anear,
And smooth Oänis' stream and land-engirdled mere,

    And grave canals and gray,
    Whereby thy Hipparis
Thy host to water finds her way.
    These palaces are his :
Like towering groves in strong array
He builds them; his inspiring might
This kindred people brings from helplessness to light.

    But ever round a master's vast emprise
    No little toil and much expense

Do battle 'gainst his work; the skies
  Are dark with risk. Yet they whose high pretence
Succeeds are counted e'en by fellow-townsmen wise.

    Lord of the clouds above,
      Our saviour, Zeus supreme,
  Long wont on Kronos' crest to rove,
      Who broad Alpheius' stream
    And Ida's solemn cave dost love,
      I come petitioner to thee
And chaunt to Lydian flutes my prayerful minstrelsy:

    This city decorate
      With fame of manly deeds.
  And, Psaumis, Oh! be this thy fate,
      Who lov'st Poseidon's steeds
    To train, and now art come elate
      With conquest from Olympia's plains,
To live a glad old age as long as life remains,

  Thy sons beside thee. Still if man possess
    Good health and spirits, and have got
    Enough of wealth, to happiness
Adding renown untarnished, let him not
Aspire to be a god in utter foolishness!

6. To Agesias of Syracuse.

As when some gorgeous banquet-hall is built
The stately porch we rear on columns richly gilt,
    So we will build : the work begun
    Must show a front resplendent as the sun.
        And if our subject be
    The winner of Olympia's victory,
Steward of yon prophetic shrines of Zeus,
And fellow-colonist of famous Syracuse,
    For such a man where can we choose
    Fit hymns in sweetest music to proclaim
His worth, whose townsmen know and envy not his fame?

    For be the son of Sostratus aware
That this his godlike fortune is.   Your merit ne'er,
    Except with peril it have fought,

In men or hollow ships with praise is fraught.
  But if with loss of ease
A daring deed is done, the memories
Of many men embalm it.   Thou the praise hast won,
Agesias, which just Adrastus long agone
    Gave to Oïkleus' prophet-son
  Amphiaraüs, when the meadow clave
And with his glossy steeds he found a sudden grave.

  When seven pyres at Thebes were finishèd
    Whereon the dead to burn ;
  Talaüs' son then cried a bitter cry ;
    And "More than these," he said,
    "The eye of all my host I mourn,
Foremost of spears in fight as first in prophecy !"
      Nor lesser laud belongs
        To Syracuse's son,
  Lord of our revels, hero of our songs.
Contentious I am not, nor strifeful overmuch ;
    But this, for I am sure of it,
  Swearing a mighty oath I will avouch.
      What I have done
  The honey-voicèd Muses will permit.

Come, Phintis, haste to yoke thy sturdy pair
Of mules, that we the car may mount, and straight may fare
    Our unembarrassed path to trace
And reach the source of this heroic race.
      Thy mules of all the rest
The road we need to take must know the best,
Who for their matchless speed upon their heads have shown
Olympia's olive crown.   To them and them alone
    Wide be the gates of music thrown !
    For I am bound to-day betimes to be
Beside Eurotas' ford by lovely Pitane.

She by Poseidon son of Kronos reaved
A child, Euadne of the blue-black hair, conceived,
    And long with folded robes she strove
To hide the fruit of her unwedded love :
      But when her hour was come,
    She sent her maids the daughter of her womb
Straight to the hero-son of Eilatus to bear,
Who in Phaisana ruled Arkadian men, and clear
    Alpheius gained by lot, to rear.
    There in her prime beneath Apollo's kiss
She first essayed the sweets of Aphrodite's bliss.

Nor aught her secret Aipytus deceived;
    He knew her babe divine;
The wrath unspeakable with anxious care
    Repressed, his soul that grieved,
    And went in haste to Pytho's shrine
To question there about the wrong he scarce could bear.
    Her purple-woven gown
    And silver pitcher she
Beneath the shelter of a thicket brown
Laid by, and there a boy divine of soul she bare.
    But Eileithuia mild of mood
And, sent by Phoibos of the golden hair,
    The Spinsters three
To help in utmost need beside her stood.

There to her painful travail's quick relief
Young Iamus was brought to light : there crazed with grief
    She left him on the earth.   But two
Protecting dragons, gleaming-eyed, thereto—
    For so th' immortals willed—
Appointed, with the harmless juice distilled
By honey-bees the infant fed.   But when the king
From Pytho's rocky cleft drove homeward hurrying,
    He bade his household, " Quickly bring

The child I know Euadne must have borne
Hither to me at once ; for Phoibos' self has sworn

Himself his sire, and promises that he
O'er all of mortal mould shall have supremacy
    In reading things divine, and ne'er
  The issue of his loins shall lack an heir."
      He spake. They all averred
With solemn phrase they had nor seen nor heard
Aught of an infant five days old. For still the child
Lay hidden in the reeds within the thicket wild,
    His tender frame with radiance mild
  Of pansies bathed of gold and purple hue :
And thence a deathless name his mother made anew

  To call him by. So when the golden crown
      Of youth was his, and all
  Her luscious fruits were tempting his desire,
      He calmly gat him down
    To dark Alpheius, there to call
Standing in middle stream upon his mother's sire
      Poseidon, ocean's lord,
      And godbuilt Delos' king
  The archer-god ; and prayed they would award

Him some folk-tending rank.   By night beneath the skies
 He cried : his sire's responsive cry
Rang quick and full of yearning, " Son, arise,
  And, following
My voice, the land where all shall come descry."

So came they to the inaccessible
Peak of the lofty mount where Kronos used to dwell :
 And twofold gifts he gave him there
Of divination, first the voice to hear
  That leasing never knew ;
And then,—when Herakles, the strong of thew
And bold in scheming, came, of all Alkaius' race
Most reverend scion, here his father's feast to place
 Where crowds the countless populace,
 And solemn games of strength,—his throne divine
Of oracles to set on Zeus' supremest shrine.

Illustrious thence throughout Hellenic land,
The house of Iamus became ; and hand-in-hand
 With honour plenty follow'd :
And holding worth in high esteem they tread
  A shining path.   The deed
Proclaims the man.   Detraction's evil meed

From others' envy hangs above the head of those
On whom the bashful Grace towards the race's close
    A glorious countenance bestows.
    Yet if in very truth, Agesias,
Thy mother's folk who dwelt around Kyllene's base

    Were often wont with prayerful sacrifice,
      In lavish piety,
    Hermes to gift, the heavenly messenger ;—
      On whom the office lies
    The games to hold and victory
Allot, the contest o'er, who counts Arkadia dear,
    The nurse of sturdy men ;—
    Then, son of Sostratus,
   'Tis he, who with his thunderous father's ken
Determines thy good luck.   I seem upon my tongue
    To feel the shrilly whetstone grate,
    That woos me nothing loth to floods of song.
      The beauteous
Blooming Metope, child of desolate

Stymphalis was my grandam, she who bare
Thebe who loves to drive the horse : whose waters fair
    I soon will quaff, and daintily

A wreath of many-tinted poesy
    Will weave for warrior-brows.
Thy fellow-minstrels, Aineas, arouse.
To maiden Hera first the shout of praise is due :
Then know if th' old reproach "Boiotian hog" we too
    With truth repel ; for thou'rt the true
    Herald, the word-stick of the fair-haired Nine,
The luscious bowl that brims with song's enchanted wine.

Be Syracuse remembered in their lays,
And rich Ortygia, which the sceptre pure obeys
    Of even-minded Hiero ;
    Who tends Persephone's gay steeds of snow,
      Demeter's ruddy feet,
    And Zeus's might in Etna's awful seat,
With welcome festive rites.   Sweet-sounding lyre and rhyme
With him are well acquaint.   Oh let not creeping Time
    Disquiet fortunes so sublime.
    May he with loving heart and kind await
The merry masque that brings Agesias in state

Back from the older toward the newer home,
    Leaving Stymphalus' walls
The mother of sheep-herding Arcady.

When far amidst the foam
Throughout a night of winter squalls
The ship must ride, 'tis well her anchors twain should be.
May heaven to these and those
Vouchsafe a bright career
In friendliness : and oh ! do thou dispose,
Husband of golden-distaff'd Amphitrite, lord
And ruler of the sea,
Their voyage straight and smooth to those aboard :
And grant me here
Th' increasing flower of winsome minstrelsy !

7. To Diagoras of Rhodes.

As when one grasps in plenteous hand
  A cup wherein the foam
Of wine's red juice is gurgling high,
  And gives it, drinking to his health,
To his young son-in-law to carry home,
Wrought all of virgin gold, the crown of all his wealth,
  The merry-making band
  Exalting, and his recent tie ;
  He renders him beside
Envied of all the friendly standers-by
  For winning a congenial bride :

So when the Muses' gift I send,
  As sweet as nectar poured,
The luscious fruit of mental strife,
  To them that wear the athlete's crown,
Men who at Pytho or Olympia warred

And won, I please them.   Blest is he whom fair renown
  And honour bright attend.
 But she who gives the bloom to life,
  The Grace, from time to time
With lyres and many a well-concerted fife
 Another victor makes sublime.

And now with both I come, and blended song.
  Diagoras beside
Rhodos the sea-girt isle to celebrate,
The child of Aphrodite, Helios' bride :
 While I shall praise with tuneful choir
The mighty man and fair in fight who wore the crowns
  For pugilistic might
Alpheius' and Kastalia's banks along ;
And Demagetus therewithal his sire,
  The friend of Right ;
Who with their Argive spearmen cultivate,
Near widespread Asia's jutting headland-tongue,
 The isle of three fair towns.

 Yes ; now will I in minstrelsy
  Aloud proclaim for them
 The story of their origin ;

How from Tlepolemus they spring,
    Branches of Herakles's mighty stem.
They boast that on the father's side direct they bring
        To Zeus their pedigree;
        And on the mother's are akin
        To great Amyntor, sons
    Of fair Astydameia.   Error in
        The speech of men unending runs.

    And hard it is to find what now
        And in the end will be
    Man's good.   For erst in Tiryns town
    The settler of this isle in ire
Struck with a cudgel of tough olive tree
Likymnius, bastard offspring of Alkmena's sire,
        And slew him with the blow,
        From Midea's chambers coming down.
        In troubles of the mind
    The wisdom of the wise is overthrown.
        So to the god at Pytho shrined

    He hied him.   From the sweet most holy place
        The god of golden hair
    Bade him equip a fleet, and from the shore

Of Lerne to the sea-girt land repair,
    Where once the sovereign king of heaven
Down on the city poured a rain of golden snow.
    What time Athene armed,
    Sprang from her father's forehead through the space
    Hephaistus' craft and brazen axe had riven ;
        And air alarmed
    Rang with her battle-cry's tremendous roar :
    Heaven shook to view the terrors of her face,
        And mother Earth also.

    Then he who light on men bestows
        The god, Hyperion's child,
    Commandment on his children laid,
        A debt of perpetuity,
    That they, the first, a splendid shrine should build
To her the goddess new-create, and solemnly
        With sacrificial vows
    Should glad the father and the maid
    Who sways the thunderous spear.
    The reverence born of Forethought man to aid
    Merit imparts and goodly cheer.

    But often deep forgetfulness,

A cloud of baffling, came
Work's path direct to lead astray,
And drive remembrance from the heart.
So bearing not the seed of burning flame
These climbed the citadel, and set therein apart
With rites no fire could bless
The holy ground.   But when the day
Was dying, Zeus supreme
Led up a yellow cloud, and rained away
Much gold : and She whose gray eyes gleam

And flash with lightnings gave them excellence
In every handicraft
O'er other toiling men : their roads were lined
With works that seemed to live and move ; the draught
Of glory was full deep.   For lore
Acquired in guileless wisdom finds a vast increase.
Men's olden legends tell,
When Zeus and all the immortals made pretence
Among themselves the earth for evermore
Divisible
To make, that Rhodos' cliffs were not defined
Above the waves, but hid from sight and sense
Below the briny seas.

But no one pointed out the share
   Of Helios far away :
They left without his lot of earth
The spotless god. He bore in mind
The slight ; and Zeus, if he had had his say,
Had cast the lots afresh ; but Helios declined.
   " Where hoar the billows are,
   Uprising from the depths to birth
   I see an isle," he said,
" Where soon shall grow a race of manly worth,
And countless flocks of sheep be fed."

Then golden-snooded Lachesis
   He bade stretch out her hand
To ratify the mighty oath
Of all the gods, and nod unfeigned
Assent to Kronos' son, that this new land
Emerging into lustrous air, while earth remained,
   Should evermore be his.
   She did his bidding nothing loth :
   The words at that dread sign
Had end in true performance. From the froth
   Of clinging saturating brine

An island blossomed.   He whom piercing rays
    Proclaim their kindred's sire
Owned it, the lord who has the mastery
Of steeds whose breath is e'en as scorching fire.
    And there in Rhodos' soft embrace
Seven sons he gat with gifts of wisest thought endowed,
    Amongst the men of yore,
  For their inheritance : in after days
  To one Jalysus, eldest of his race,
    Kydippe bore,
  Kameirus next, then Lindus.   These in three
Their father's land dividing, went their ways
    And each his own abode

Called by his name.   There sweet amends
    For sorry hap in life,
  As to a god, is offered now
  To Tiryns' prince Tlepolemus
With sacrifice of sheep and manly strife.
And there Diagoras was twice victorious ;
    Where Isthmus seaward trends
  Four times ; where Nemea's olives grow
    Twice running he has ta'en
The crown ; and where from her steep mountain-brow
    Athene gazes on the main.

The Argive shield his grasp has known :
   And Thebes, and Arcady,
The yearly games Boiotians hold,
Pellene too, his peerless fame
Have echoed back : Aigina's victory
Six times he won : the tale of him is still the same
   On Megara's graven stone.
   Zeus father, who does guard the wold
   Of Atabyrius' height,
The customary hymn in honour hold
   That celebrates Olympia's fight,

And him whose goodly fist has gained the prize.
   And modest reverence
From fellow-townsmen and from strangers grant
To him : for aye a foe to insolence
   He treads his honest path : for he
Has throughly learned the truths that from good ancestors
   Have grown within his soul.
Kallianax's seed from kindred eyes
Hide not away. Whene'er the Eratidæ
   Are graced, the whole
City with festive cheer is jubilant.
But oft while sunshine still illumes the skies
   The rising tempest roars.

8. To Alkimedon of Aigina.

MOTHER of contests crowned with crowns of gold,
     Mistress of Truth,
All hail! Olympia, where the prophet-priests of sooth
    Around the burning victim stand,
       Intent to find
     Some index of the mind
Of Zeus, who holds the vivid levin in his hand;
  If he have word of them whose souls are manned
Thy wreath to win, and rest from labours manifold.

  And answer oft rewards the piety
     Of them that pray.
Thou leafy grove of Pisa nigh Alpheius' spray
    This masque and show in gracious mood
      Accept; for great
     Is always his estate,
Who wins thy splendid prize of manly hardihood.

Yet not to all men comes the selfsame good.
The gods have many paths to reach prosperity.

And thee, Timosthenes, thy fate
Assigned to tutelary Zeus, and he,
Who in the Nemean ring gave thee renown,
    Now to Alkimedon
By Kronos' mountain-crest allots Olympia's crown.
    Right fair to look upon
He was, nor have his deeds his looks belied,
    When in his wrestle's victory
He named Aigina's isle his native state,
    Whose long oars sweep the sea,
Where saviour Themis stranger-shielding Zeus beside

Sits in exceeding worship.   What is much,
    And is inclined
In many ways, 'tis hard to judge with righteous mind
    And opportune.   Yon little land
    Amid the brine
    By some decree divine
Was set, a blessed column of defence to stand
    For every stranger.   Oh ! may heaven command
That through the time to come it still may aye be such.

By Dorians held since death the sceptre broke
    Of Aiakus ;
Whom Leto's Phoibos and Poseidon glorious
    Summoned, when they on Ilium
        To rear were bent
        A crown of battlement,
To help them build the wall.   For cruel wars would come,
    And 'midst the city-sacking battle's hum
Its stones, so Fate had willed, must breathe devouring smoke.

    There three gray dragons at a tower,
    When first 'twas builded, leapt : whereof the twain
Fell back and yielded up in dire alarm
        Their souls at once : the third
Passed hissing in.   Apollo marked the sign of harm,
        And straight took up the word
    Of warning, " Hero, where those hands of thine
        Have wrought shall Pergamus be ta'en.
    So speaks the hostile portent of this hour
        To me in language plain,
Sent here by Kronos' son, the thunderer divine.

    Yet not without the aid of thy descent
        All this shall be :

Thy very children of the first and fourth degree
   Shall lead the foe." He spake, and sought
      His Xanthus' banks,
     And th' Amazonian ranks
Well-horsed, and Istros; whilst the trident-wielder brought
  Their fellow here to Isthmus' ridge sea-wrought,—
And fast the golden steeds that drew his chariot went,—

  And Corinth's precipice, his famous feast
    To witness there.
Nothing to all men seems in equal manner fair.
    Should I in song rehearse the praise
      Melesias
     From beardless striplings has,
Her ruthless stone against me let not Envy raise.
   Like honour, I declare, in former days
In Nemea's lists he gained, and later pancratist

  Was hailed where grown men strove. The man
  Who once himself has learned, more easily
  Can teach: to shirk instruction marks the fool:
    For inexperience
Is light of heart, but they whose selves have been to school
    Have better competence

To point the method which may best advance
    Him, who the proud celebrity
Is fain t'achieve of wreaths Olympian.
    Melesias, for thee
The thirtieth honour this, Alkimedon's good chance.

    Favoured by luck divine, yet not deprived
    Of manliness,
Four young competitors his blows' terrific stress
    Sent hating their abasement home,
    With shame-tied tongue
    To live unknown to song :
And in his father's sire new vigour caused to come,
    Wherewith to combat eld and brave the tomb.
He seldom thinks on death who pleasantly has lived.

    But sleeping Memory I must arouse
    To tell the tale,
How aye the Blepsiad race was wonted to prevail :
    For whom with conquest surfeited
    The sixth green crown
    Of contest is put down.
And part of their renown to those to Hades sped
    Is duly given.   Dust hides not from the dead

The cherished honours gained by scions of their house.

So when he hears the joyful tale
From Gossip, Hermes' daughter eldest-born,
Will Iphion Kallimachus advise
How Zeus upon their seed
Has just conferred the world-renowned Olympic prize.
So ever meed to meed
Still let him add, and sharp diseases fend!
I pray of their prosperity
He bid not adverse Nemesis avail;
But that their city he
May with themselves exalt in peace until the end!

9. To Epharmostus of Opous.

ARCHILOCHUS's strain,
　　Olympia's song,
The shout of 'Conquering Hero' thrice renewed,
　　Sufficed for Epharmostus, when
　　Before the friendly train
He led the revels Kronos' hill along.
　　But now with mightier dart
Sped from the distance-killing bow-string of thy Muse,
　　Approach, my heart,
　　The solemn throne of Zeus
　　Who hurls the levin red as blood,
And yonder sacred mountain-peak the pride
　　Of Elis' country-side
　　Acquired by Peleus, erst the flower
　　Of Lydia's men,
His bride Hippodameia's fairest wedding dower.

Then loose thine arrow's wing
   So sharp and sweet
At Pytho. Lay not hold of words that bend
  Earthward, when thou preparest to wake
    Thy cittern's quivering
To hail the man who rival wrestlers beat,
    The son of great Opous ;
Mingling his praise with hers, whom Law, and Ordinance
     Her glorious
    Daughter,—so fell the chance,—
  With saving presence aye defend.
And nigh Kastalia's fount in fame she grows,
   And where Alpheius flows,
  Whence primest garlands brought of late
    More honoured make
The forest-shaded mother-town of Lokris' state.

And I, for fain I am the town I love
  With burning song to cause to shine,
Swifter than noble steed or wingèd ship can move
  Will blazon east and west and south and north
    This joyous rede ;
  If by the hand of Destiny
  The Graces' chosen garden-close be mine.

For theirs is every pleasant meed.
   'Tis only heaven's decree
That mortal men endues with wisdom or with worth.

   Else how had Herakles
     His cudgel whirled
In triumph o'er the trident, when before
   His Pylos' walls Poseidon fought
    And gave him little ease ;
When Phoibos, silver-bowed and golden-curled,
    In battle pressed him hard ;
While Hades shook in wrath that dread mysterious rod,
    Wherewith toward
   The hollow pathway trod
   By all the dead in years of yore
He guides the newly-slain.   My mouth, refrain
   Thy words : so rash a strain
   Abjure : the lore that gods decries
    Is ruin-fraught ;
And boasts inopportune with madness harmonize.

   Such babble put thou down :
    And let alone
All strife and warfare of the deathless ones.

Attune thy tongue to celebrate
    Protogeneia's town,
Where by command of Zeus Deukalion
    And Pyrrha, from the crest
Of cold Parnassus coming, made their first abode
    Wherein to rest,
    And rear a race that owed
    Its origin to fleshless stones
And not to nature, telling in its name
    The source from which it came.
    For these song's speeding breath upraise :
    And ancient date
For wine, for minstrel's work the newest blossoms praise.

Once on a time, they say, the mighty force
    Of waters deluged sombre earth ;
But through the Thunderer's skill back to its briny source
    Was driven to make precipitate retreat.
    And thence descent
    Your brazen-shielded sires could trace
From old Iapetus, whose blood at birth
    With all the noblest ichor blent
    Of Kronos' heavenly race :
A constant line of kings in their ancestral seat.

Before Olympus' lord
Unhindered caught
Opous' fair daughter from th' Epeian land
Up to the ridge of Mainalus ;
And there upon the sward
Enjoyed her charms, and her to Lokrus brought,
Lest age should slay him, bare
Of children, doomed to die alone.   The wife in time
A sturdy heir
Brought forth ; with joy sublime
The son committed to his hand
Lokrus beheld ; and 'twas by his desire
That for his mother's sire
They called the child ; to manhood grown,
A marvellous
Hero in look and deed : to whom his folk and town

His father gave in charge.
To him a host
From Argos, and from Thebes, and Arcady,
And Pisa gathered : every guest
With bounty free and large
He welcomed, but Menoitius honoured most
Of all the stranger band ;

The child of Aktor and Aigina, whose one son,
　　When Teuthras' land
　　Th' Atreidæ reached, alone
　Stood with Achilles manfully,
　When Telephus repulsed the Danaan troops
　　Home to their galleys' poops ;
　　To show the wise what courage fired
　　Patroklus' breast.
Whenceforth the hero born of Thetis' womb required

　That never 'midst the cruel battle's roar
　Patroklus should consent to stand
Save where Achilles swayed his conquering spear before.
　Borne in the Muses' car a nobler lay
　　'Twere mine to make,
　Full power with courage following.
But for Lampromachus I sought this land,
　For valour's and his friendship's sake
　　His Isthmian wreaths to sing,
Where either held the lists through all one livelong day.

　And two successes more
　　At Corinth's gate
Were theirs, and oft was Epharmostus' head

In Nemea's valley crowned : a boy
Proud Athens' bays he wore ;
Triumphed a man at Argos.   Oh ! how great
His honours bourgeoned, when
Leaving the beardless crowd of youths at Marathon
To rival men
The silver cup he won !
With never-stumbling, stealthy, tread
And nimble turn he passed his elders by;
And oh ! with such a cry—
The course completed—took his meed ;
Radiant with joy,
Bright with the bloom of youth, and fair with fairest deed !

And 'mongst Parrhasia's throng
How wondrous fair
He showed him at Lykaian Zeus's feast,
And at Pellene, when his corse
He mantled with the strong
Warm remedy for winter's chilly air.
And Iolaüs' tomb,
Seabeat Eleusis too, for witnesses have seen
His laurels bloom.
Whate'er is best, I ween,

Is nature's work ; yet some at least
Of men by taught accomplishments acquire
    The glory they desire :
  But what is done apart from God
      'Twere none the worse
To leave unhymned to silence.   'Tis not every road

  That leads an equal length ; nor thrive we all
    By one pursuit ; yea learning's hill
Is steep to climb.   But since to grace this festival
  Thou bring'st thine offering, sweet Muse of mine,
      Be bold and cry,
  That he with strength of hand was blest
And supple limbs from birth by heaven's will,
    And courage flashing from his eye,
      Who late at Aias' feast
Oïleus' honours gained, and crowned the hero's shrine.

10. To Agesidamus of Epizephyrian Lohris.

THERE is a time when men stand most in need
Of breezes fair; a time when most for rains they long,
Cloud's stormy children : but by toil if one succeed
 He finds his recompense in dulcet song,
The source of future tales, the faithful augury
Of fame that ever waits on mighty deeds gone by.

And these ungrudgèd songs of praise are given
To all Olympia's victors : these my tongue to tend
Is fain, as shepherds tend their flocks, for aye from heaven
 The blooms of poet-lore to men descend.
Know then, Agesidamus, yea, be well assured,
Son of Archestratus, thy prowess has secured,

 Besides the golden olive's diadem,
  A crown of honied song which I will weave,

Regardful of the race of Lokrians of the West.
 Then haste, ye Muses, haste, to lead with them
  The revels : I will guarantee
 No stranger-hating people ye shall find,
  No dullard folk of brutish mind,
But shall a highly-cultured race of warriors see :
For never fiery fox nor roaring lion leave
 The characters by Nature's hand imprest.

11. To Agesidamus of Epizephyrian Lohris.

OH ! read me where within my wit
  The name of him who won Olympia's bough,
    Archestratus's son, is writ ;
For erst I promised him the sweet reward of song,
      And now too long
My promise have forgotten.   Gentle Muse, and thou,
  Great Zeus's daughter, Truth, from Pindar fend
  The blame of having lied and wronged a friend.

With shame of all my depth of debt
  The days then future, now left far behind.
    Come up to cover me : and yet
Vantage of interest may cancel slander's score.
      When billows hoar
Roll backward, who may some far-whirling pebble find?
  And where will be the people's carping mood
  When payment whelms reproach in gratitude ?

For Justice over Western Lokris sways
The rod of honest rule : her people cultivate
Kalliope and brass-clad Ares.   Rumour says
    That e'en the wondrous thews of Herakles
Were foiled at first by Kyknus.   Thanks for help so great
To Ilas let Agesidamus, decorate
    With Pisa's boxers' chaplet, give as gave
    Patroklus to Achilles.   Prodigies
Heaven's hand with training works in one by nature brave.

    But few except with toil attain
That gladness which can most a life illume.
    The oracles of Zeus constrain
Me now to hymn the strife of all the strifes beside
        The chiefest pride,
Which stalwart Herakles nigh Pelops' ancient tomb,
    Established, when his strong right hand had slain
    Fair Kleätus and Eurytus, the twain

    Sons of Poseidon : so to get
His labour's wage from haughty Augeäs,
    Bent to exact the scouted debt.
So in a coppice dense beneath Kleonæ's gate
        He lay in wait,

And suddenly o'ercame them in the way ; whereas
   Ambushed in Elis' mountain-passes they
   Had once his Tiryns' army made their prey ;

   O'erweening offspring of Molione !
And very soon the Epeians' guest-defrauding king
Beheld his country, rich with long prosperity,
   And his own city, sinking in the stream
Of such calamity as sword and fire may bring
When foemen smite and spare not.   'Tis no easy thing
   Strife with a stronger force to set aside :
   And Augeäs, misled by folly's dream,
Knew first the captive's chains, and then dishonoured died.

   To Pisa then the mighty son
  Of Zeus his booty brought and all his train :
   And for his sire, the peerless one,
A holy precinct measured out, and fenced around
     In open ground
Our consecrated Altis, and the circled plain
   To rest and feasting after toil assigned :
   And dark Alpheius' stream in honour joined

   With the twelve sovereign gods ; and bade

Men call the steep by Kronos' name, that erst
 Had borne on an untitled head,
The while Oinomaüs reigned, the snowy winter gear
  Of many a year.
And when these solemn rites by him were stablished first
 The Fates were stationed at the founder's side,
 And he by whom alone the Truth is tried,

 Unerring Time: who now in later days,
How Herakles the first-fruits won in war among
The gods in sacrifice distributed, displays:
 And how for every fifth recurring year
He organized the first Olympic feast with song;
And valour's prizes gave amid th' assembled throng.
 In wrestling, running, racing, tell me who
 Conceived in thought the wish away to bear
The contest's fame, and gained by deed the garlands too.

 Oionus first, Lykymnius' son,
 From Mideä came—her army's chief—and he
 With ease the furlong footrace won:
In wrestling Echemus the honours of the brave
  To Tegeä gave:
And where the pugilists encountered, victory

Fell to Doryklus, who of Tiryns' land
Was denizen : with horses four-in-hand

    The son of Halirrhothius,
  Samus from Mantineia, bore away
    The prize : with spear victorious
Phrastor the target struck : Enikeus put the stone
      Far off alone
With skilful twist of hand ; a long and loud hurrah
  His backers raised.   And fair Selene's ray
  With lovely light lit up the dying day.

    Then all the sacred field was flooded o'er
With song at gladsome feasts according to the use
Of Pisa's country-side.   And we the ways of yore
  Will follow now ; the hymn of victory
We too will raise ; and we the olden theme will choose,
The fiery-handed levin hurled by thundering Zeus,
  The burning bolt that fits his boundless might :
  Whilst with the dulcet reed in harmony
Soft notes of song shall wake the echoes of the night ;

    Song that by Dirke fair of fame
  Sees light at last though all too long delayed.
    And as a son to bear his name

Born of his wife, the child of long and fond desire,
    With love's sweet fire
An aged father's bosom warms ;—for wealth uplaid
  For a strange lord of alien ancestry
  Is bitterness to one who soon must die ;——

   So he who noble deeds has wrought,
  But comes to Hades' gloomy home unsung,
   Has spent his days in toil for nought
Save momentary joy ; but now the sweet-toned lute
    And dulcet flute,
Agesidamus, honour's prize to thee have flung.
  And wide-spread fame your favour companies,
  Zeus' gifted daughters, fair Pierides !

.And I my hearty zeal with theirs combine
Illustrious Lokris' state with warm embrace to greet,
Steeping in honied praise her children's noble line :
  Archestratus' belovèd son elate
To praise, whom I beheld beside the holy seat
Of great Olympia's god in pugilistic feat
  Succeed ; who fair in face as brave in deed
  Had then the bloom of youth, which shameless Fate
Erewhile, with Kypris' aid, repelled from Ganymede.

12. To Ergoteles of Himera.

I PRAY thee, child of Freedom-giving Zeus,
    Protecting Fortune, keep
Good watch o'er Himera's strong walls ; for thine the hand
    Across the pathless deep
  That guides the course of wingèd ships ; on land
That sudden wars controls, and rules deliberate
    Councils of state.
For human hope unreal phantasies pursues,
Now tossing high, now low, athwart the waves of Fate.

  Nor ever presage true of future fare
    Did one of mortal kind
Find from the gods.   Their hints of coming destinies
    To us are always blind ;
  And expectation oft event belies.
Without a note of warning unalloyed delight

    Will take her flight :
And they, whose barque the storm has sorely tried, despair
Exchange in little time for joy's supremest height.

    Son of Philenor, e'en thy speed of foot,
      Like barndoor cock that only fights at home,
        Had perished fameless, void of fruit,
Beside thy native hearth, had no sedition come
      And set thy Knossus' citizens at strife
        And robbed thee of thy home and ease.
      But now thy forehead wears Olympia's crown ;
      And, Pythian garlands twice, Ergoteles,
      And Isthmian won, thou liftest to renown
The Nymphs' hot baths, where thou dost lead thy farmer's life.

13. To Xenophon of Corinth.

WHILE I extol the family
Whose temples Pisa's wreaths have thrice been seen to twine,
   To townsmen kind, to strangers generous,
       My song shall celebrate
       Corinth the prosperous,
       Isthmic Poseidon's gate,
Far-famed for children fair.   There Order loves to bide
With two twin sisters—safe foundations of the state—
   Justice and Peace, who wealth to man divide ;
       The golden progeny
Of one who never errs in council, Right divine.

       And Peace and Justice love to fend
Presumption, loud-mouthed mother of Satiety.
   An honourable tale is mine to tell ;
       And honest hardihood
       My tongue would fain impel

To speak.   What in the blood
Is born, 'tis vain to strive to cover.   Oft on you,
Aletes' sons, the flowery Seasons have bestowed
   The glory sacred games on might of thew
      Confer, within your mind
Oft sowed the seed of ancient ingenuity.

   The merit of device
      Is his alone
Who first conceived it.   Tell me, then, from whence appeared
   The joyous feast of Dionyse
   With bullock-guerdoned dithyramb ? and who
His chariot first with reined and bitted horses drew?
   Or on th' immortals' temples reared
   The king of birds in double shape of stone ?
      The Muses too
   Here sweetly breathe ; and Ares here
Beholds with glee the lads who wield the deadly spear.

   O father Zeus, whose boundless sway
Unrivalled rules Olympia, aye ungrudging be
   To these my hymns, this people at their ease
      Preserve, and waft thou on
      With favourable breeze

The barque of Xenophon.
For him the chant, that lauds his prowess' meed, receive,
Which he from Pisa's plain is bringing, having won
  The wreaths that foot-race and pentathlon give,
    And both within one day:
No mortal e'er before had such prosperity.

    And chaplets wove of parsley twain
His tresses covered when to Isthmus' games he sped ;
  And Nemea utters no discordant sound.
    Alpheius' stream beside
    The legends still abound
    For what a light, swift, stride
His father Thessalus was known.   At Pytho he
In single course and double e'er the daylight died
  Triumphed : with three fair wreaths of victory,
    Before one moon could wane,
His locks swift-footed Day at Athens garlanded.

    Hellotis' feast seven times
      Beheld him win ;
And where Poseidon's course on either hand the sea
    Assails, embalmed in grander rhymes
    With Terpsias' and Eritimus' name,

His father Ptoiodorus, on the scroll of fame
    Inscribed, shall ever deathless be.
  I dare the world to tell how often in
      The Delphian game
    And Lion's close the bell ye bore.
'Twere easier to count the stones on ocean's shore.

    But everything has fitting bound,
Which only the best time reveals.   To themes of state,
   Chanting the prowess of the dead, when I
      A private man proceed,
      In nothing will I lie
      Concerning Corinth's meed,
Famous for wisdom as for warfare.   There was bred
Wise Sisyphus whose craft the gods could not exceed ;
  And there, against her father's bidding wed,
      Medeia came, who found
Escape for Argo's keel and saved her living freight.

    And when by force before the walls
Of Dardanus the armies thought on either side
   To end the war ;—with Atreus' kindly son
      One bent to bring again
      Sweet Helen home ; and one

To rid their native plain
Of foreign foes ;—the Danaan chieftains shook to see
Glaukus from Lykia come.   " A very wide domain
   Beside Peirene's city," boasted he,
      " And royal banquet halls
Were once my father's own, and kingship far and wide."

   He by the fountain-head
      Intent to break
The snaky-tressèd Gorgon's offspring Pegasus,
    Had oft ill-hap encounterèd;
   Ere to his side the maiden Pallas went
Bearing a bridle trapped with gold. His dreams were spent
    At once in vision.   " Sleep'st thou thus
   Prince sprung from Aiolus," the goddess spake,
      " Arise attent,
   Take this to spell yon stallion's fire,
A white bull slay, and show this to thy taming sire."

   Sleeping he saw at midmost night
The Virgin of the deep blue shield come near and speak
   These words.   At once he leapt upon his feet ;
     The marvel by his side
     Took up, and glad as fleet

In happy hurry hied
To seek his country's seer, old Koiranos's son,
And show him all his chance, and how at eventide,
   As he had bid, the goddess' steps upon
      He slept, and in his sight
The maiden born of Zeus, whose wrath the thunders wreak,

   Produced the soul-subduing gold.
And Polyidus bade him instantly fulfil
   The vision ; to the earth-encompasser
      The strong-foot's neck to lift
      In sacrifice, and her,
      Equestrian Pallas, gift
With altar new. Beyond man's utmost hope or vow
The potent arm of heaven has often raised his thrift.
   And round the wingèd horse's muzzle now
      Bellerophon the bold
The taming spell applied, and joyed to see his will

   By such a steed obeyed.
     Triumphantly
He mounted him, and all his paces sportive tried,
   In brazen coat of mail arrayed.
With him the Amazonian ranks he fought

Of female archers from the airs bare bosom fraught
    With icy blasts : before him died
  Chimaira breathing flame : the Solymi
      By him were brought
    To nought.   His fate unsung I leave :
The ancient stalls of Zeus on high the horse receive.

    But whilst my whirling darts I reach
Straight at the mark, I must not all my strength of thew
  Misuse, the many far beyond to throw.
      For it has been my fate
      Right willingly to go,
      The Muses throned in state
And Oligaithus' stalwart offspring vowed to aid,
To Isthmus and to Nemea.   Still I will relate
  Much in a tale as short as may be made.
      Full sixty times at each,—
The herald's welcome voice shall be my witness true,--

    They won.   In Pisa what their fare
Has been already told, methinks. What yet shall be
  I then will clearly tell ; at present I
      But hope ; with those above
      The future issues lie.

Would that the kindly love
That guarded all their race may further persevere !
To Zeus and Ares this we leave the task to prove.
How often on Parnassus' brow, and near
Argos, and Thebes ; and where
Lykaios' kingly shrine shall bear to Arcady

Witness ; at Sikyon,
Pellene too,
Eleusis, Megara, the well-defended grove
Of Aiakus ; rich Marathon,
Euboia ; 'midst the towns that 'neath the crest
Of Etna thrive in beauty ; they have been confessed
Unmatched ! Their crowns though Hellas rove
To count ; they beggar knowing. Monarch, who
Canst grant request,
Smooth passage give o'er life's rough sea,
And temper triumph's sweet delights with modesty.

14. To Asopichus of Orchomenus.

Ye graces three,
Ye queens of minstrels' singing, who frequent
The charger-breeding lands of fat Orchomenus
That has her lot beside Kephisus' waters clear,
Ye warders of the olden Minyæ,
When I implore you, hear!
For yours is all delight,
Yours all that renders life for mortals sweet or bright;
And if a man
Be wise, or fair, or valorous,
The gift is yours.   Without your stately aid
Nor solemn feasts nor blithesome dances can
The gods immortal celebrate:
But, stewards of the mysteries on high,
Your seats in seemly state
The golden-bowed Apollo, Pytho's lord, anigh
Are evermore arrayed,

For hours in ceaseless praise of Zeus Olympic spent.

O worshipful
Aglaia and Euphrosyne, who love
The sounds of song, ye daughters born to Zeus the king
Of gods themselves, my invocation hear; and thou,
Thalia, who dost music's blossoms cull,
On our procession now
Look kindly as it goes
To render thanks for good success on tripping toes.
In Lydian style
Asopichus I came to sing.
Through thy deserts the Minyeian town
Is hailed Olympia's winner.   Haste the while,
Echo, to reach the sable walls
Where dwells Persephone; his father tell,
Whom Hades' converse calls
Kleodamus, gladsome news, in Pisa's famous dell
How his young son half-grown
Her wingèd honours wreathed his flowing locks above.

PYTHIAN ODES.

1. To Hiero of Syracuse.

My golden cittern, whom
  Apollo keeps
In common with the raven-tressèd Muses, thee,
    Beginner of the revelry,
  The dancers' step awaits ; the minstrel choir,
  When thy sweet strings' melodious quivering
    The prelude wake, thy signs inspire
The hymn that ushers in the festival to sing.
Zeus' pointed bolt of fire eternal thou in gloom
  Canst shroud ; the eagle on his sceptre sleeps,
    And lets his wide
Pinions so swift of flight droop down on either side ;

    Of all the feathered kind
      Though he be lord.
About his beakèd head a cloud of sable night
    Thou sheddest ; o'er his orbs of sight

Spelled by thy sweep of song his eyelids close

In pleasant slumber ; softly to and fro

   He sways his back in deep repose :

Nay, headstrong Ares' self has oftentimes let go

His lance's cruel point with sleep to glad his mind.

  To souls of gods thy missiles calm afford,

      With skill endued

By Phoibos and the Muses' full-clad sisterhood.

     But whosoe'er

Of Zeus's love have never had a share

    Are sore distressed

To hear the cry of the Pierides .

On land or midst the dark resistless seas.

Like him who lies in baleful Tartarus,

Typhoeus of the hundred heads, the deadly foe

   Of all the gods, whom erst

   Kilikia's famous cavern nursed :

But now the sea-beat cliffs precipitous

  That frown o'er Cumæ hold him down,

And all Sikelia weighs upon his shaggy chest ;

  And Etna's pillar-peak that pierces air,

     With ice bestrown,

   The yearlong nurse of nipping snow :

From whose recesses jets
    The awesome flood
Of fire that none may near; and while the daylight beams
    A cataract of smoke that gleams
    With lurid lights her torrents pour, but when
    The dusk of even falls, her blaze blood-red
    Rolls boulders huge each ragged glen
Adown, to splash and sink in ocean's level bed.
'Tis yonder reptile born to lame Hephaistus lets
    These fountains forth.   To all the neighbourhood
        A prodigy
Of fear and wonder full he is to hear and see ;

    And how the plain between
        And Etna's crest
Of dark-leafed forest he is chained, and all his back
    The torments of his bedding rack
    Laid out at length.   O Zeus, I pray thee grant
    That I may find acceptance in thine eye ;
    Who lov'st this mountain-top to haunt,
A fruitful country's front, whose namesake city nigh
Her famous founder has bedecked with glory's sheen ;
    Since Pytho's herald on the course confessed
        Her honours thro'

The chariot-race's crown adjudged to Hiero.

By those who sail

Across the seas 'tis deemed of prime avail,

When they begin

A trip, to quit the port with breezes fair :

For thus 'tis like that they will home repair

With better luck : so in my song of praise

For this success I fain would find an augury

That many a future year,

For steeds' victorious career

And crowns and feasts and hymns that minstrels raise,

Renown on Etna may attend.

Oh ! Lykian Phoibos, Delos' king, delighting in

Kastalia's fount in steep Parnassus' vale,

Do thou befriend

This noble land, and hear my plea.
    (

For human excellence

From heaven derives

All means of growth, and none, unless the gods assent,

Is wise or strong or eloquent.

And Hiero to laud is my intent ;

So hope I that my missile may not fall

Without the lists, as javelin sent
From whirling hand with cheek of brass, but distance all
Opponents by its cast.   Would heaven the affluence
   And gifts of wealth's increase wherein he lives
      May ne'er be less ;
While Time of anguish past affords forgetfulness.

   Or brings to mind instead
    The memory
How boldly in the stress of fight he held his own ;
   When at the hands of gods a throne
  They gat, an honour such as Hellene ne'er
  May reap, the diadem of majesty
   And unexampled wealth to wear.
And now forsooth in Philoktetes' fashion he
Has gone to war, and one that held a haughty head
  Has found it need his flatterer to be.
    They say of yore
The godlike heroes came from Lemnos' lonely shore

   The archer-son
Of Poias, by his ulcer nigh undone,
   To fetch away ;
Who wasted Priam's city, and at length

The Danaans' labours ended, poor of strength
Although he went, for thus it was decreed.
So may the healing god vouchsafe to Hiero
    In coming time to be,
   Granting him opportunity
To gain whate'er his heart of hearts may need.
   Before Deinomenes upraise,
Sweet Muse, the pæan of the four-in-hands, I pray ;
  For children share the joy by father's won.
     Then bid our lays
   For Etna's sovereign friendly flow ;.

    Since Hiero for him
     Resolved to rear
That town in freedom 'neath the laws of Hyllus' rule.
   For in Aigimius' Doric school
  The sons of Pamphilus and Herakles—
 Who 'neath the slopes of wild Taÿgetus
   Are settled, dwelling at their ease—
Have ever wished to bide.   With fortune prosperous
They quitted Pindus' clefts in ages distance-dim,
  Amyklæ gained, and dwelt in glory near
     The snowy steeds
Of Leda's twins, abloom with fame of warlike deeds.

Grant, Zeus who hearest prayer,
    In years to come
That kings and citizens by Amenanus' burn
    May truth from falsehood aye discern.
  Let Hiero a guiding-star arise
  His son to lead, his folk in honour hold,
    And both in quiet harmonize.
I pray thee, Kronos' son, their warcry overbold
Let not Phoinikian nor Tyrrhenian foemen dare
  To shout again, but keep them still at home,
    And ponder well
The lamentable loss that all their fleet befell

    At Cumæ when,
  By Syracuse's lord subdued, their men
    He bade to throw
Forth from their speedy ships into the sea ;
And from the heavy bonds of slavery
  All Hellas freed.   From Salamis the fame
Of Athens I will chant for meed ; the deadly fight
    At Sparta sing, that nigh
  Kithairon's heights was fought, whereby
The Persian host of bent-bowed archers came
  To ruin ; while to laud the kin

Of great Deinomenes my hymn of praise shall flow
  Of deeds in Himera's well-watered glen
    Achieved, wherein
    Their enemies were put to flight.

    If at the season meet
     One lift his voice
Twisting his many threads to one diminished strand,
    Less hard will be man's critic-brand
  Of blame ; for evermore satiety
  Tarnishes eager hopes : a townsman's ears
    Do ne'er so much in secrecy
Weigh down his soul, as when a friend's success he hears.
Yet pass not honours by, for envy is more sweet
  Than pity. Guide with honest helm the choice
    Of yonder throng :
On Truth's good anvil forge the arrows of thy tongue.

    For if a syllable
     Of folly fall
Out of thy mouth, 'tis deemed of moment, being thine :
  Thy every good or evil sign
  A host of trusty witnesses observe :
  Of many people thou hast stewardship.

Thy native bloom of heart preserve ;
And if thou lovest to have thy praise on every lip
Shrink not from spending : loose the sail that breezes swell,
   Like wary skipper.   Be not snared withal
       By cozening cheats.
'Tis posthumous renown that tongue to tongue repeats

       Alone may show,
   Dear friend, the life of mortals hence who go,
       By minstrelsy
  And story-tellers' faithful histories.
  The kindly worth of Kroisus never dies ;
  And Phalaris, of the burning brazen bull
And cruel mind, has earned an infamous renown
      Wide as the world, and ne'er
    Do tuneful citterns let him share
  Their joyance when the banquet-hall is full
   Of carols of the gentle train
Of boys. The first of prizes is prosperity,
  The second good repute ; but he, below
     Who both may gain
   And keep, has won the highest crown.

2. To Hiero of Syracuse.

O Syracuse, thou mighty capital,
Domain of Ares deep in schemes of war,
        Thou nurse divine
Of men and steeds that joy in brazen gear to shine,
        From wealthy Thebes I come
        To bear my sonnet home,
That tells the triumph of the four-horse car
Earth-shaking, well-appointed, wherewithal
        The crown, whose jewels glow
        The farthest, Hiero
Round his Ortygia's head rejoiced to twine ;
The seat of Artemis the river-maid,
        Without whose aid
His gentle hands had striven in vain
To tame the horses reined with many-coloured rein.

For she, the arrow-loving maid, confers
By help of Hermes, lord of every game,

With both her hands
Effulgent graciousness on him ; with harness-bands
    When to the chariot gay
    And wheels that aye obey
  The rein he yokes his steeds of mighty frame ;
And on the potent trident-brandisher's
    Assistance calls. The meed
    Of song for noble deed
Of kingly worth for kings of other lands
Have other poets fashioned. Kinyras
      Full often has
   His Kyprus' minstrelsy inspired ;
The cherished priest of Aphrodite's altar, sired

  By golden-haired Apollo's tender love.
    For pious gratitude
    Repaying deeds of good
Thereto impels. But thee, son of Deinomenes,
  The maiden sings in Lokris of the West
    Before her doors, for through thy power
    She dwells in safety at this hour,
From helpless terrors freed of threatening enemies.
    Obeying the behest
      Of gods above,

Bound on his wingèd wheel, they say,
That whirls for ever every way,
Ixion cries to men, " Oh make it your delight
Whoe'er to you is kind with kindness to requite."

And dearly too the lesson he had learned :
For when he lived with Kronos' gracious kin
    A life of bliss,
The surfeit of success in pride he took amiss ;
    And madly passion-led
    Aspired to Hera's bed,
The joyous bed that only Zeus may win.
But insolence to guilt surpassing turned
    His heart, and speedily
    In matchless anguish he
Met his deserts. A twofold crime was his
That wrought the pains, which evermore accurst
    He bears : that first
    Of mortal race in kindred blood
His hands, and not without deception, he imbrued ;

And next that in her chambers vast and dim
The bed-fellow of Zeus he durst assail.
        Sore need it is

That each should see the bounds of his capacities.

> For lawless marriage ties
> In ceaseless miseries

Have often plunged their seeker.   Hark the tale.

A phantom of enjoyment cheated him ;

> For, knowing not his case,
> He clasped in love's embrace

A cloud whose form assumed the symmetries

Of Kronos' heaven-enthronèd child.   The wile

> Him to beguile

The hands of Zeus contrived, and pain

In beauty masked : and so Ixion gat a chain

> Through wheel-spokes four enwound for his despite ;

> A living death ; and there,
> In fetters he shall ne'er

Escape, the message he received to bruit abroad.

But she—no kindly Grace at hand appeared—

> A lonely son produced alone,
> A monstrous wight, who never shone

In company with man nor feared the laws of God ;

> But by his mother reared,
> Kentaurus hight,

With wild Magnetian mares would lie

On Pelion's wooded spurs, whereby
A wondrous army sprang to life, whose figures show
Both parents' likeness, sire's above, and dam's below.

God to accomplishment alone can bring
His every hope ; god, who can overtake
    The eagle's wing,
And pass the dolphin by when fastest traversing
    The ocean's vast expanse,
    And human arrogance
Can humble in the dust, and others make
For ever famous.   Fain would I the sting
    Of deadly slander flee.
    For I have seen, though he
Died long ago, how oft to wandering
His evil-speaking drove censorious
    Archilochus,
    Battened on bitter words of hate.
Where wealth and wisdom meet is man's most blest estate.

And such a lot, illustrious prince, is thine,
In thoughts of liberality displayed ;
    Whose sovereign sway
Many a host and well-embattled town obey.

And if it be averred

That Hellas ever heard

Of hero in the olden days, arrayed

In wealth and honours that would thee outshine,

 Such vain contention is

 But utter foolishness.

My galley flower-decked I'll mount to-day

Chanting thy excellences. Courage rife

  For battle strife

 Becomes a youth; and I declare

Of such distinction thou hast found a boundless share;

Now in the ranks where rival chariots strove,

  'Mid serried footmen now.

  And smooth although thy brow

Thy counsels that might suit with grizzled tresses free

My path from danger when thy praise I sing.

  Then hail! Across the hoary sea

  This festive lay I send to thee

Like merchandize of some Phoinikian argosy.

  Be willing, gracious king,

   To meet with love

  My gift of Kastorean words,

  Set to Aiolian music's chords,

For this my seven-tonèd cittern's sake ; and be
What thou hast learned thou art.   Let children beauty see

   In monkey-tricks, and shout their loud 'huzzas' :
  But Rhadamanthus lasting happiness
      Has gained, for he
Possessed a spirit void of all iniquity,
     And ne'er delighted in
     Deceptions from within,
  Such as are born of whisperers' finesse.
The secret tales of slanderers, alas !
     Are double-edged for ill,
     Like foxes' natures.   Still
What gains this gainsayer's malignity ?
Though sunken all the fishing-gear may be
      Deep in the sea,
   Yet like the cork above the net
I float upon the waves, and am not even wet.

  A fraudful townsman's word must ever lack
  Weight with the good.   Yet fawning everywhere
     He'll surely try
Each cunning twist he knows.   Not such an one am I
    In impudence.   I love

To friends a friend to prove :
A foe to foes, I hold it not unfair
Now here now there by crooked paths to track
    Their feet in wolfish guise.
    The man who always tries
Straightforwardly to act, and hates a lie,
Advances every rule ; or be it thrall
    Monarchical,
    Or clamorous mob-government,
Or wise men's statesmanship. 'Tis well to rest content

With God's decision, who will now uplift
    The one, and by-and-bye
    Superiority
To others give. But this arrangement pleasures naught
    The jealous souls : their vast ambitions draw
    Too long a line, and in their heart
    Plant many a wound of painful smart,
Ere they attain the end of all their anxious thought.
    The yoke of present law
    As heaven's gift
    To bear as lightly as he can
    About his neck is best for man.
'Tis slippery travelling to kick against the goad.
Welcome amongst the good be ever my abode !

3. To Hiero of Syracuse.

Oh would to heaven,
If my poor voice may speak the common tongue's refrain,
Life from the dead were given
To Cheiron son of Philyre,
Ouranian Kronos' mighty seed.
Amongst the glades of Pelion again
In majesty to reign ;
A wildwood brute to look upon indeed,
But souled with all a man's humanity ;
Such as he was when he of old Asklepius nursed,
Soft anodynes' kind author, first
To give relief to pain's severest smart
And bid disease depart.

Him ere the child
Of Phlegyas the horseman bore, her latest throe
Assisted by the mild

Midwifely Eileithuia, she
    Went,—on her bed of travail slain
By shafts from Artemis's golden bow,—
    To Hades' home below :
Apollo planned her end.   The enmity
Of Zeus's children never wakes in vain.
And she in waywardness had slighted him, and wed
    Another suitor, though her bed
Without her father's knowledge she had shared
    With Phoibos flowing-haired,

And bare his fruit divine within her womb.
Yet chose she not the festival to wait
That welcomes new-wed brides, nor list the mingled cry
    Of hymeneal revelry,
Which comrade maidens of a like estate
    With serenade delight to come
    And carol when the sun is set :
    But craved a something lacking yet.
    Not seldom thus it is :
    There is a tribe of men that scoff
    At present good and peer far off
    In search of future bliss ;
Insensate fools, who hunt with zeal

And hopes that no fruition feel
Unreal phantasies!

And such a blind
O'erpowering spirit of bewilderment possessed
Fair-robed Koronis' mind.
A stranger came from Arcady;
And she to his soliciting
Gave ear: the sin was not without attest:
For at his own behest
Great Loxias himself, her temple's king,
At sheep-receiving Pytho chanced to be;
And from his fellow true, his own prophetic soul
Omniscient, he learned the whole;
Who never lies, whom never god nor man
Deceives in act or plan.

Where Ischys, son
Of Eilatus, had lain when he became aware;
And how the wrong was done
By fraud, his sister dread, with wrath
Resistless boiling o'er, he sent
To Lakereia. For the girl did bide
Boibiis' banks beside.

Another god procured her punishment,
   Turning her footsteps to an evil path.
And many of her neighbours shared her fate, and died
    With her; as on the mountain side
  Fire from a single spark has oft been known
     To burn a forest down.

But when her kinsmen on the wooden wall
  The damsel laid, and all around it shone
Hephaistus' greedy fire with many a leap and jet,
    Then spake Apollo, " I not yet
  Have heart to bear that offspring of my own
    So piteous ending shall befall,
    Because his hapless mother died."
  He spoke.   With one tremendous stride
    The blazing pyre he clomb;
  The flames to either side were cleft,
  As quick the babe unborn he reft
    From his dead mother's womb :
  Whom to the Kentaur straight he bore
  To Thrace, to learn the healing lore
    That rescues from the tomb.

    There all who came—

Though long companionship with sores self-nurtured
    Had gnawed away their frame,
     Or cold gray steel, or massive stone
     Had struck by some far slinger slung,
    Or summer's heat or damps by winter shed
      Their strength had minishèd—
This way and that he rid of pain ; he sung
Soft strains of incantation over one,
Gave others soothing draughts, and healing salves around
    The aching limbs of others bound ;
  And some whose wounds were quite incurable
     He made by cutting well.

      But evil greed
Of gain has captive made even Philosophy.
     And for a mighty meed
      E'en him did proffered gold persuade
    From Hades' realm to bring again
A man whom Death had ta'en. But speedily
     His bolt of destiny
   The son of Kronos hurled with might and main
  Through both their breasts, and took their breath, and dead
Bright lightning healer laid and healed. At heaven's hand
    No mortal e'er should more demand

Than mortal heart befits; the fact should see,
    And what is our degree.

Affect not, sweet my soul, in froward pride
A life that knows no end, but manfully
Do what thou find'st to hand.   If prudent Cheiron dwelt
    Still in his cave, and I could melt
His heart with honied hymns' soft melody,
    I now had won him to provide
    Some son of Phoibos or his sire
    For godly folk to cool the fire
      Of fever's suffering ;
    Who dark Ionia's boisterous sea
In swiftest barque should cross with me
    To cure my friend the king,
    Who reigns in Etna's citadel,
    Beneath whose walls the waters well
      From Arethusa's spring.

    Right royally
His Syracuse he rules, to all her citizens
    Full of benignity ;
    Not envying good men's renown.
    To strangers kind as sire to son.

Could I have come empowered to dispense
    The double recompense
Of golden health and song of prizes won
At Pytho, adding splendour to the crown
At Kirrha gained by Pherenikus' victory;
    Then over yon abyss of sea
More radiant had my coming's brightness been
    Than heaven's starry sheen.

    But I will pray
The Mother whom, with Pan, the maids before my door
    Address in night-long lay,
    The solemn goddess.   Hiero,
    If thou hast skill to read aright
The sum of saws, thou knowest well of yore
    From wise men gone before
The deathless ones on mortals in their spite
One benefit are wonted to bestow
For two mishaps; and fools this limited success
    Can hardly bear with seemliness:
The good know better, making it their pride
    To show the brighter side.

Thee happy fates attend: for greatness aye

Looks on a king who guides his people's choice
More than on other folk.   But bliss without a flaw
    Nor Aiakus' son Peleus saw,
Nor godlike Kadmus, by the common voice
    Though happiest of men were they ;
    Who heard the Muses sing upon
    The wooded sides of Pelion
    With golden-snooded head,
    And seven-gated Thebes within :
    Where one was blest enough to win
    For partner of his bed
Harmonia of the splendid eyes ;
And one the child of Nereus wise,
    Illustrious Thetis, wed.

    With both of them
The gods had feasted : both the progeny had seen
    Of Kronos' royal stem
    King-like on golden thrones present
    Their wedding-gifts.   From labours past
They rested, and they made their hearts serene
    Through grace of Zeus : but teen
Most sharp a little later overcast
And robbed of all his share of merriment

The one, through sore mishaps that all his daughters three
    Involved in sorest misery —
    'Twas father Zeus himself who visited
      White-armed Thyone's bed.—

      The other's child,
In Phthia whom immortal Thetis bore alone,
      When by the arrow stilled
      His spirit fled amid the war,
      Wrung, as he burned upon the pyre,
  From Hellas' host an universal moan.
      But if a man have known
The way of truth, he still should more desire
That heaven may prosper him.   Inconstant are
The breathings of the winds that sport beneath the sky;
      And thus with man's felicity,
    When most the tide is running full and strong
      It will not tarry long.

    Lowly in lowly case, and great in great,
    Will I be.   I will alway reverence
The fortune that attends me most religiously
      With all my means; but, if to me
    The gods should ample store of wealth dispense,

Good hope have I that decorate
With high renown my name will go
To after folk.   We Nestor know,
    Lykian Sarpedon too,
By tales in sounding song set forth
Which skilful wrights have fashioned.   Worth
    Becomes eternal through
Illustrious poesy.   But they
Who thus achieve an easy way
    To glory are but few.

4. To Arkesilas of Kyrene.

A cherished friend to-day
Thou must arouse thee to attend, my Muse,
  Well-horsed Kyrene's king;
That with Arkesilas's revelling
  Thou mayest speed upon its way
The gladsome breath of sacred carol due
  To Leto's children two,
And Pytho, where the priestess erst,
Who sits beside the golden birds of Zeus,
While Phoibos stood anigh, proclaimed that Battus first
  Should fruitful Libya colonize,
And quit his holy isle, and bid a town,
Whose charioteers should gain a glorious renown,
  Above her chalky hill arise:

  And brought to mind again,
When generations seventeen were gone,

The word Medeia spake
At Thera, when Aietes' daughter brake
 Her silence in a deathless strain.
Thus Kolchis' fiery princess cried unto
  Warlike Iason's crew
 Of sailor demigods, " Ye seed
Of gods, and men of mettle every one,
Hearken ! From this seabeaten land it is decreed
 That in the days to come shall rise
A child of Epaphus, a daughter fair,
To plant the germ of towns adorned with human care
 Within Zeus-Ammon's boundaries.

  Short-finnèd dolphins there
They shall exchange for horses fleet, for oars
 Shall handle reins, and chariots drive
Whose wheels shall thunderous be as whirlwind-storm.
  That this shall be their fare,
 And Thera shall the mother city be
  Of many a powerful colony,
That omen is the pledge which, where the lake out-pours
 For Triton named, the god in human form
  Was resolute to give ;
The clod, which from his prow as host-gift to receive

Euphemus lighted down, and such good hap
Zeus, Kronos' son, affirmed with lucky thunderclap.

Just as the sailors weighed
The anchor checked with brass, quick Argo's bit,
He came beside.   Before
For twelve long days our ship from Ocean's shore
We carried, where no grateful shade
Earth's desert ridges tempered.—This design
To beach our craft was mine.—
'Twas then the lonely god appeared,
His form and every feature shaped to fit
The semblance bright of one whom all of us revered;
And some few friendly words addressed
To usward, such as hosts benevolent
Who make a feast are wont to speak of kind intent
To every fresh-arriving guest.

But our unfeignèd pleas
Of eagerness to reach our own sweet home
Precluded stay : then he
Eurypylus professed himself to be,
Son of divine Ennosides
The earth-encircler.   He could understand

Our haste.   With his right hand
He grasped at once a lump of clay
Where he was standing, as it chanced to come,
And friendly sought to give it : not to say him Nay
Euphemus straightway leapt ashore,
And hand from hand received the clod divine.
Which from our ship, I hear, was washed, and in the brine
Was whelmed amid the billows hoar.

At dusk of eventide
It happened in the watery main to sink.
Yet oft had I on all enjoined,
Who shared my toils, to guard the treasure well :
My care was nullified
By their neglect.   And now th' immortal seed
Of boundless Libya, ere 'twas need,
Bestrews this isle.   For if at home, by Hades' brink,
To Tainarus' god-guarded citadel
The clod had been consigned
By him the ocean-king of steed-subduing mind
Poseidon gat, Euphemus, whom of yore
Europa, Tityos' child, beside Kephissus bore ;

His sons of fourth degree
H

Had with their Danaan kindred occupied
 That wide-spread continent.
For then had happed a vast self-banishment
 From Lakedaimon's chieftaincy,
And from Mykenai, and from Argos' bay.
  But now, alack the day,
 In foreign arms he must beget
A chosen race who, when they shall have hied
God-helped to Thera's isle, in ages distant yet
 Shall sire the man predestinate
 To lord it o'er the plains of sable cloud ;
Whom Phoibos in his house with wealth of gold endowed
 Shall warn in oracles of fate

  At once from Pytho's shrine
 To go, and afterwards his host in ships
  To lead across the sea
 To Kronian Neilus' fertile boundary."
 Such, slowly uttered line by line,
Was dread Medeia's prophecy ; and they,
  The demi-gods, her lay
 Of lore sagacious moveless heard,
 And held their breath in awe with silent lips.
O blessèd son of Polymnestus, that one word,

Spoke by the Delphic prophet-bee
With unsuggested cry, thus welcoming
Thee thrice, 'All hail !' proclaiming thee the fated king
   Of rich Kyrene, righted thee :

   When thou wert questioning
What recompense th' immortals would demand
   To cure thy speech so blurred and lame.
And ever since and still, as in the height
   Of purple-blossomed spring,
Eight generations of thy children thrive ;
   And Phoibos now and Pytho give
Arkesilas, from all that dwell around her land,
   Th' applause wherewith her chariot-race is dight ;
   And him intent I am
To dedicate unto the Muses, with the ram
   Of golden fleece, for that the Minyæ
Sought, when there rose for them divine celebrity.

   What cause to sail the sea
Was theirs ?   What peril's nails of adamant
   Bound them the quest to try ?
The gods had said that Pelias should die
   Through the illustrious progeny

Of Aiolus, by schemes inflexible
    Or force. The oracle
  Of freezing purport, uttered next
    The shady mother's central radiant,
Came back and ever back in dreams, and sorely vexed
     His anxious soul, "On every hand
    The single-sandalled watch with strictest care ;
Should such an one come down from lofty mountain-lair
    To famed Iolkos' sunny land,

    At once a citizen
  And foreigner." And so he came at last,
    A wondrous man to view,
  With javelins twain, and double garments too :
    One, which Magnetia's countrymen
  Wear, fitted close his shapely limbs within,
    And one, a leopard-skin,
  From shuddering tempest shelter gave :
Nor were his curling tresses shorn nor cast
Away, but down his back fell rippling wave on wave.
    And straight with swift unflinching pace,
  To make of his undaunted spirit test,
The market-place he sought, and stood where thickest pressed
    The city's rabble populace.

They recognised him not ;
But one of them that gazed in wonder said,
    "This man can scarce Apollo be ;
And yet he is not Aphrodite's spouse
    The brazen-carred, I wot ;
And, story tells, in Naxos' vineyards' shade
    Iphimedeia's sons are laid,
Otus, and thou, O bold king Ephialtes, dead.
    And Tityus, all the common talk allows,
      An arrow suddenly
Brought down, from Artemis' unconquered sheath set free :
    To teach that none should dare to aim above
What he may fairly reach, who dreams the dream of love."

    And so they gossiped on
With mutual response, till Pelias
    In polished wagon placed
Mule-drawn arrived in hurry's headlong haste :
    And as his vision lit upon
The well-known sandal bound about one foot
    Alone, with horror mute
He sat awhile ; then strove to hide
The fear within his heart. "What country as
Thine own dost thou pretend to, stranger guest ?", he cried

" What hoary-locked old woman bare
Thee on the earth?   With lies that all detest
Defile not thou thy mouth, but from a truthful breast
The story of thy birth declare !"

Boldly the youth replied
In gentle accents, " Cheiron's lore I bring :
For from his cave I come,
From Philyre's and dear Chariklo's home,
Where holy maids, the Kentaur's pride,
My childhood nurtured whilst I was a child.
But now that I've fulfilled
A score of years—nor word nor deed
Dishonest ill-repaid their nurturing—
I have come home to claim again the ancient meed
Of honour which my father bore,
Where others now by means iniquitous
Bear rule, the throne which Zeus conferred on Aiolus
And on his sons in time of yore.

For Pelias, I hear,
Gave rein to pallid thoughts of jealousy,
And stripped by fraud and violence
My royal parents of their olden right ;

And they in deadly fear
Of that o'erweening tyrant's wanton mood,
When first in newest babyhood
I saw the light,—while all the maids a doleful cry
Set up, and all the house with mourning dight
Assumed a vain pretence
Of grief for one just dead,—in secret sent me hence
Wrapped in my crimson cradle-clothes, my guide
The starlit night, to grow at Kronian Cheiron's side.

Now that my history
Ye know in brief, O trusty citizens,
As clearly tell me where
My parents lived, who used to drive their pair
Of milk-white steeds.   Not strangerly
I tread a foreign soil, but, Aison's child,
Come home ; and yonder wild
Brute-shapèd being half divine
Iason named and called me 'mongst his glens."
He spake.   And, as he came anigh, his father's eyne
Saw and acknowledged him, and then
The tear-drops through his agèd eyelids welled
For joy of heart that he his darling son beheld
Grown up the handsomest of men.

Hearing the glorious cheer
Aison's two brethren joined their gathering,
    One Hypereia's well
Leaving, and one Messene's citadel—
    This dwelt far off, and that anear—
Pheres and Amythaon, and with them,
    A sprig of either stem,
    Admetus and Melampous made
Their cousin welcome.   He with banqueting
And gracious words received the festive cavalcade,
    All kindly hospitality
Providing fitly.   Five long days and nights
In all good fellowship they culled the sweet delights
    Of unrestricted revelry.

    But on the sixth new day
To all his kin the lad with earnest word
    His story from the outset told.
They all assented : quickly from his seat
    With them he took his way
To Pelias' abode, and therewithin
    Impetuous they stood.   The din
When he, the lovelock-wearing Tyro's offspring, heard,
    He came at once his visitors to meet.

And then Iason bold
In gentle language all his counsel 'gan unfold,
A sure substructure laying first whereon
Wise words to build.   " Rock-sundering Poseidon's son,

The minds of men are swift
Successful craft to justice to prefer ;
Although they know the sting
They meet with in the morrow's reckoning.
Come then, do thou and I uplift
Our souls to higher laws, and reining wrath
Work for ourselves a path
Of happiness.   My tale I tell
To one that knows it.   Kretheus was of her
Born, who the resolute Salmoneus bare as well :
And we their third descendants see
The golden sun in glory.   Ill-content
The Fates withdraw, where those of one descent
Quarrel, for very modesty.

'Twould ill beseem us twain
The mighty honours of our ancestry
With brazen swords and spears
To dissipate, the gains of olden years.

So I agree that thou retain
The sheep, the yellow herds of beeves, the lands
   Which from my father's hands
   Thou took'st and now dost cultivate,
Swelling thy wealth—nor aught it vexes me
That these illicit gains enrich thine old estate—
   So thou on thy part be not loth
The royal wand and throne, where Aison sate
His knightly people's strifes by law to regulate,
   Without renewed distress to both

   To render us again,
Lest some fresh evil hap thereout arise."
   Thus spake Iason. Tyro's heir
As gently answered, " As thou sayest I
   Will be : but all the train
Of age's ills already me attend :
   With thee the bloom of youth, my friend,
Is just at flood, and thou the ire canst neutralize
Of those beneath the earth. For Phrixus' cry
   Bids us in haste repair
To far Aietes' realm, and thence his spirit bear
   Back home, and fetch the ram's long-hairèd fleece,
By which from angry seas he once obtained release

And from the godless aim
Of his step-mother's darts.   A vision fair
Comes, and addresses me
In this strange manner.   I to Kastaly
To seek of her diviners came
If aught were there revealed.   And there they bade
A ship at once be made,
And me to sail it.   This decree
If thou consent to perfect, I will swear
To pass the throne and all my kingly power to thee.
Let Zeus this pact of ours attest,
A mighty witness, guardian-god of both."
They all then went their ways having affirmed the oath.
But brave Iason hot for quest

His heralds far and wide
Dispatched his instant sailing to proclaim.
And quickly heroes three
Came to him, Kronian Zeus's progeny,—
And two were lovely Leda's pride,
The other restless-eyed Alkmena bore,—
All tireless men of war.
And other twain with crested locks,
The seed of dread Ennosides, there came

From Pylos and from Tainarus' projecting rocks,
    Half-shamed because they were so strong,
    Euphemus clept and Periklymenus
The stalwart-thewed : and, sprung from Phoibos, glorious
    Orpheus, the lyrist, sire of song.

    Twin brothers Hermes sent,
  Who wields the rod of gold, the toil to share
    Throughout.   Echion one was hight
The other Eurytus, both brimming o'er
    With youth and merriment.
And swiftly they who dwelt about the root
    Of far Pangaius followed suit,
Zetes and Kalaïs. With willing, cheerful, air
  Their father Boreäs, who rules the roar
    Of stormy winds, for fight
Equipped them well, and both about their backs were dight
  With purple feathers. Hera stooped to fire
The demi-gods with such o'erpowering sweet desire

    Of Argo's crew to be,
  That none would stay behind to pass his days
    At home in sodden ease
From danger free, but e'en to death would seize

The fairest meed of bravery
Amid his fellows.   When the peerless host
To rich Iolkos' coast
Came down prepared to dare the sea,
Iason told them o'er with words of praise.
And Mopsus then, the seer well skilled in augury,
In gladness his prophetic tongue
Unloosed, and by the birds and lots divine
Bade all aboard.   But when the anchors o'er the brine
Well lashed above the beak they hung,

The chieftain on the poop,
Clasping a golden bowl betwixt his hands,
Gan call on Zeus the sire
Of th' heavenly race, who wields the lance of fire,
And on the speed-imparting swoop
Of waves and winds ; and favourable days
And nights and watery ways
Implored, and, all success to crown,
The blessèd lot to see their native lands
Once more.   From out the clouds in thunder came adown
Auspicious answer : brilliantly
The lightning-flashes through the welkin broke :
These signs of heaven's assent the heroes trusting, took

Therefrom fresh energy; and he,

The portent-gazer, cried
" In with your oars," and pleasant hopes held out.
Then stroke on stroke there followèd
The toil of hands that plied the ceaseless oar;
And o'er the foaming tide
By southern breezes wafted speedily,
The inlet of th' Unfriendly sea
They reached, and for marine Poseidon fenced about
A consecrated close : some roving score
Of Thrace's bullocks red
Beside an altar grazed but newly finishèd
With hollow top of stone : and there they prayed
The lord of ships, or ere the danger they essayed,

That scathless they might flee
The furious onset of the Clashing Rocks.
For islets two there were,
Alive, and each on other wont to bear
With headlong rush more speedily
Than ranks of roaring winds. That vessel fraught
With demigods had brought
Their doom. But when to Phasis' shore

The heroes came, it cost a few good knocks
On Kolchis' dusky folk well-planted, when before
        Aietes' self they came.   And she,
    Who owns the barbèd shafts that sharpest sting,
Down from Olympus brought the wryneck, leg and wing
        Bound on the wheel that none may free.

            The Kypriot deity
    First gave that painted crazy bird to men ;
            And spells of prayer and lay
    Taught Aison's prudent son, to take away
            Medeia's virgin modesty,
    And reverence to sires by children due,
                And plant her heart anew
        With longing, burning, mad, desire
    Of Hellas through Persuasion's urging.   Then
She showed him all the tasks of strength with which her sire
        To test his prowess purposèd ;
    And gave him, mingled with his wrestler's oil,
An antidote for harms ; and promised, when his toil
        Was over, she with him would wed.

            But when Aietes pressed
        Into their midst the adamantine plough,

And brought the bulls, whose yellow jaws
For breath exhaled a flame of burning levin,
    Whose brazen hoofs' unrest
Smote clanging on the ground alternately,
    Beneath the yoke unaided he
Led them ; and drove them straight as if by measure through
  The meadow's loamy back : the share was driven
    A fathom's length.   Applause
Followed.   Then spake he, " If the king, who gives his laws
  To ships, this work of mine can end to-day,
Then let him take yon wearless coverlet away,

    Yon fleece with golden wool
Resplendent." When he stopped, his saffron cloak
    Iason doffed, and bold
In heavenly aidance on the work took hold.
  Through his wise hostess' wonderful
Behests the fire had lost its power to vex :
    And round the bullocks' necks,
    Seizing the plough right manfully,
  He cast and made secure compulsion's yoke,
And on their vasty flanks the goad incessantly
    Applied ; and thus by violence
  The task assigned the youth completed. Low

Aietes groaned within himself to see it so,
  Jealous of such omnipotence.

    But all his company
  Reached to such courage hands of friendliness,
    And gathered off the ground
  The fragrant meadow herbs, whereof they wound
    Him wreaths, and spake him lovingly.
  And then the wondrous son of Helios
    Told how the luminous
  Skin still was lying where the knife
Of Phrixus stretched it out.   And ne'ertheless
He hoped that task would cost the stranger youth his life.
    For far within a coppice laid
  By an enormous dragon's teeth 'twas held,
Whose length and bulk a ship of fifty oars excelled
    By blows of iron mallets made.

    Along the broad high way
  Far might I travel ; but my hour is nigh.
  A pathway short I know full well
Most other bards surpassing in this lore.
    His arts availed to slay
  The gray-eyed serpent with the mottled skin,

l

Arkesilas, and with it win

Medeia not unpleased, who Pelias to die

   Betrayed.   And thence they gained the Ocean's shore,

      And past the Red Sea's swell

' To Lemnos' island came, whose women, strange to tell,

   Their lords had slain, and there for garments wove

In feats of manly strength and hardihood they strove,

    And consorts took at will.

  And then on foreign soil the fated days

    Or nights received the seed

Of your oncoming glory : bright indeed

   Its primal radiance shone, for still

The race new-planted by Euphemus there

    For evermore is fair

    From age to age ; and later, blent

With Lakedaimon's sons' more hardy ways,

To th' island styled of old 'the Lovely Isle' they went :

   And thence to you the Libyan plain

The son of Leto gave to hance, and spread

The honours of the gods, and o'er the city, head

   Of golden-throned Kyrene, reign ;

   For ye the paths had found

Of prudent counsels.   Now the wisdom learn
    Of Oidipous, I pray.
If from a huge old oak one lop away
  The branches stretching far around
With sharpened axe, and all its beauty mar :
    Though leafless, fruitless, are
    Its limbs, yet witness still it shows
Of its old nature ; if at last to burn
In winter fire it comes, or, where the columns' rows
    Lift lordly heads upright, the weight
  Supports of all the miserable style
That decorates the walls of foreign owners, while
    Its ancient place is desolate.

    A mediciner thou art
Most opportune, and Paian holds thy light
    In honour.   He a gentle hand
Should bring who tends a suppurating wound.
     'Tis but a coward part
And lightly played to set a state at odds ;
    But oh ! 'tis hard, unless the gods
Consent beyond their wont to guide the helm aright
  For them that rule, again to render sound
    A plague-afflicted land.

Yet such a lot for thee by special grace is planned,
   Arkesilas.   Oh be it thine to dare
On thy Kyrene's weal to lavish all thy care.

    Do thou consider too,
  And put in practice, this Homeric saw,
    " A worthy messenger
  On every matter honour will confer."
    So to my Muse shall now accrue
  Honour from worthy message.   Long was known
    Throughout Kyrene's town
    And Battus' most renownèd hall
  How well Demophilus obeyed the law :
For whilst among the lads he still was young yet all
    His counsels showed the practiced sense
  Of elders who a hundred years have lived :
Ill tongues of all their loud assurance he deprived,
    And hatred learned of insolence ;

    Nor ever 'gainst the good
  Strove he, nor wasted time with long delay.
    For opportunity
  Is slow to come for men and swift to flee ;
    And well he knows her fickle mood,

And waits on her, her henchman not her slave.
　　The worst of griefs men have
　　Is happiness to know, and be
　Therefrom by cruel fate shut out, they say.
Far from his father-land and all his property
　　He like another Atlas now
　Is struggling with the heavens.　But deathless Zeus
The Titan host released.　Their canvas sailors loose
　　When once the storm has ceased to blow.

　　And still he hopes and prays
　That, when he shall have drunken to the dregs
　　The bitter cup of misery,
　Once more he may behold his home ; and, where
　　Apollo's fountain plays,
　May oftentimes when brims the flowing bowl
　　To youthful joyance give his soul ;
Or, bearing on his arm his lute of many pegs,
　Contented converse with the wise may share,
　　Nor plotting injury
Nor harmed of others.　There perhaps he'll tell how he,
　Arkesilas, has found a fount for thee
Of song divine, when late in Thebes a refugee.

5. To Arkesilas of Kyrene.

STRONG is the sceptre riches sway,
When Fortune puts them in the way
    Of mortal man,
With virtue never soiled by slip
To dwell in loving fellowship ;
    And since thy childhood 'gan
Its baby steps, above the rest,
Arkesilas, thou hast been blest
    With both by lot divine :
And glory's palm is thy reward
Through Kastor's aid the golden-carred ;
Who after winter's tempests dark and drear
Has bid thy hearth rejoice with happy cheer
    And bright sunshine.

But even gifts th' immortals send
The wise apply to better end :

And on thy road
Of justice thou art compassèd
With much success ; for thou art head
Of countries great and broad,—
Because thy born nobility,
This rank most reverend on thee
Imposing, occupies
Thy very soul ;—and further still
Because by Pytho's famous hill
Thy steeds have had the bliss the prize to gain,
And from thy people now thou hear'st the strain
Of triumphs rise,

Wherein Apollo joys.   So ne'er forget,
Whilst thou art hymned in thy Kyrene's lays
Round Aphrodite's garden sweet,
For all success the god to praise.
And in thy friendship let
Karrhotus hold preëminence of place ;
For not excuse he brought,
The child of tardy-minded After-thought,
Returning to the home of Battus' royal race ;
But, nigh the stream of Kastaly
Where rival chariots meet

Made welcome, with the meed of victory,
 A garland fair,
 Has bound thy kingly hair :

 Which in that famous course he won
 Where circles twelve are swiftly run :
  Nor, when 'twas o'er,
Did splintered wood or damaged rein
Or harness chafed betray the strain :
 But all the work he bore,
That dextrous smiths had wrought of old
With ivory inlaid and gold,
 And crossing Krisa's hill
In Phoibos' hollow glen he hung :
Close by the man that bowmen sprung
From Krete set in Parnassus' temple, hewed
From one big block, a beam of cypress-wood
 Upholds it still.

 So must thou one, who heaps on thee
Renown, receive benignantly
 With willing mind.
And thee, Alexibiades,
Those lovely-tressèd goddesses,

The Graces, have combined
To make illustrious.   And blest
Thou art, from grievous toils to rest,
   And get from poet's hand
   Unequalled song's memorial:
   Because, where forty met their fall,
Thy dauntless courage drove thy car safe home ;
And thence to Lybia's plain thou now art come,
     Thy fatherland.

None is nor has been nor shall ever be
Without his share of toil.   Yet Battus' race
   His old good luck has follow'ed
   In evil as in happy case ;
   A tower of majesty
To citizens, a light of clearest ray
   To strangers.   Him before
The lions fled for fear with sullen roar,
When sounds unknown he brought them o'er the salt sea-spray.
   'Twas Phoibos, who his army sent,
   That gave the beasts to dread ;
Lest for Kyrene's master ill event
   Should falsify
   His gift of prophecy.

He from disease's sorest smart
To men and women can impart
   Relief; he brought
The lyre to earth ; he grants the Muse
Of song to whomsoe'er he choose ;
   He stills unruly thought,
And wins the bosom strife-distrest
To gentleness and law and rest ;
   He haunts the mystic cave
Whereby in Lakedaimon's towers,
In Argos, Pylos' heavenly bowers,
He set the stalwart seed of Herakles,
And old Aigimius' sons.   The mightiness
   Of Sparta's brave

Engraved upon the roll of fame
Is mine ; for thence my fathers came,
   For Aigeus called,
To Thera by the god's advice ;
And there the festal sacrifice
   Some fate anew installed ;
And thence we too received the rite,
Karneian Phoibos, who to-night
   In this thy festival

Extol well-built Kyrene's charms ;
Which strangers clad in brazen arms,
Antenor's Trojans, held, who hither came
With Helen, having seen in smoke and flame
    Their country fall

The prey of Ares.   Full of gladness they,
Hasting with sacrifice and offering,
  Received the knightly company
  Whom Battus guided, opening
    The deep sea's pathless way
For his swift-wingèd ships ; and first he made
    For all the host divine
A wider precinct round a statelier shrine ;
And then a straight-cut road with level paving laid
    For steeds to trample, when men wend
    Apollo's surgery
Imploring.   There beside the forum-end
    In lonely pride
    They laid him when he died.

Long as he lived on earth with men
He lived in happiness, and then
    Was worshippèd

By all his folk as demi-god.
But, each before his own abode,
  The other royal dead
In holy calm apart repose,
And, while the stream of song bestows
  Its soft refreshing dew
On deeds of wondrous daring, hear
In heart in that their nether sphere
Their common honour and the grace their son
Arkesilas right worthily has won ;
  Who 'midst the crew

Of youthful choristers must sing
Praise to the golden-sworded king
  Of Pytho, whence
The conqueror's triumphal hymn,
His costs' reward, has come to him.
  Him all the folk of sense
Applaud.   His mind and tongue excel—
'Tis but the common tale I tell—
  His years.   In bravery
A wide-winged eagle 'midst a flight
Of fowls, a very wall in fight
Unyielding, on the wings of song he soared

In childhood ; now his wisdom reaps th' award
    Of victory

In Delphi's chariot-course.   Undaunted he
Has dared each road to reach his people's praise.
  Some kindly god has perfected
  His powers now.   In after days,
    Ye blessèd Kronidæ,
Grant him in counsel wise as strong in thews
    To live, that so no blast
Of Autumn's chilly tempest overcast
And spoil his later time.   The sovereign will of Zeus
    Directs the luck that waits upon
    Those he has cherishèd.
And him I pray that great Olympia soon
    May guerdon with
    Her garland Battus' kith.

6. To Xenokrates of Akragas.

I BID ye hearken : for we turn again
The harvest-field of Aphrodite restless-eyed,
    Or of the Graces, whilst we press
The rock-hewn centre-stone to reach of noisy earth ;
    Where for the wealthy house of Emmenes,
And stream-fed Akragas, and most for thee, Xenokrates,
    The Pythian victor's chiefest pride,
A store of deathless song, is piled in readiness
    Beside Apollo's gold-adornèd hearth :

Which neither all the storms of driving rain,
The ruthless army ranked in winter's roaring skies,
    Nor hurricane of winds shall drown,
Bruised by rough shingles tossed beneath th' unresting sea
    Down in her deepest depths. But it shall tell,
With countenance that gleams with light unquenchable,
    What, Thrasyboulus, glorifies

Thy sire and all his kin, the charioteer's renown
    Of conquest gained in Krisa's coombs by thee.

And while with skill of hand from every foe
Thou win'st the prize, the just command thou keepest whole,
    Which once the son of Philyre
On Peleus' stalwart child among the hills, they say,
    Enjoined when sireless left. "Thy praise award
To deep-toned Kronides above all gods, the lord
    Of levin-flash and thunder-roll;
Nor e'er from parents while their fated weird they dree
    Take this, the homage of thy hands, away."

Just such a disposition years ago
Stalwart Antilochus inspired, who died his sire
    To save, abiding the attack
Of Memnon, Aithiopia's slaughter-loving chief.
    For one of his two horses, pierced from far
By darts from Paris' bow, encumbered Nestor's car,
    And brandishing his spear in ire
The old Messenian saw his foeman press his track,
    And hailed with troubled soul his son's relief.

Nor fruitless fell to earth his loud appeal;

But on the spot that man of more than mortal clay
    Stood still, and purchased with his life
His sire's escape.   His prodigy of work complete,
    He seemed of young men in the time of old
The palm for filial devotedness to hold.
      Those good old days have passed away ;
But Thrasyboulus 'mongst the lads that now are rife
    Our fathers' honoured standard best could meet ;

Who pressing close upon his uncle's heel
Has showed his splendour.   Yet to prudence he subdues
     High fortune ; prone to cultivate
Nor youth's mad lawlessness nor supercilious ease,
    But wisdom where the Muses' coverts be.
And still his loving soul, Poseidon, cleaves to thee,
     Earth-shaker, who wert first to use
The harnessed steed.   With friends his sweetness is more great
    Than perforated comb of toiling bees.

7. To Megakles of Athens.

IMPERIAL Athens! with thy name I best may 'gin
 To build the basement of my lofty song,
  That lauds Alkmaion's sturdy kin
 For horsemanship. What country or what house
   More glorious
Could poet name amid this earth's unceasing din
  To thrill Hellenic tongue?

For wheresoe'er the town be, 'tis a household word,
 The honour of Erechtheus' populace,
  Who have thy holy shrine restored
 In sacred Pytho beautiful to see,
   Apollo. Me
Thy conquests and thy fathers'—five on Isthmus' sward,
  One in Olympia's race,

  Surpassing, Zeus-conferred, and two

At Kirrha—lead to hymn thee, Megakles.
And much thy new success doth please
    Me ; still I rue
That envy will not all thy merit spare
    To cross.   But, so they say,
Such stedfast, flourishing, success alway
    Must good and evil bear.

8. To Aristomenes of Aigina.

O kindly Rest,
Thou child of Law, in whom the thriving state is blest,
Who hast the keys
Supreme of council as of war,
Deign to accept for Aristomenes
The Pythian winner's honours. Thou
Of ample knowledge art possessed
When best the seasons fitting are
To act the gentle part or suffer it, and how.

But whensoe'er
One drives into his heart a grudge that will not spare,
Indignantly
Thou meet'st the onset of the foe,
And layst his braggart powers in the sea.
Unduly when Porphyrion

Provoked thee, he was unaware
How sore a fate he challenged so.
That gain is sweetest which from willing homes is won.

But violence
E'en the vainglorious sort
In time will overthrow ;
The sin Typhoeus would not shun,
Kilikia's monster of the hundred heads,
Nor yet the Giant-King.   And so they perished, one
By Zeus's bolt, and one by Phoibos' bow :
Who greets Xenarkes' son
With kind benevolence,
From Kirrha coming girt with conquests' meeds,
Parnassus' bays and Doric sport.

The Graces' hand
Cast not away in scorn yon honest sea-girt land,
That long has nursed
The virtues of the glorious
Aiakidæ ; but perfect from the first
She holds her fame.   For often she
Is hymned by the triumphal band,
When in the strife victorious,

The battle of the swift, her hero progeny

Success attain :
Wherefore her fame is high for men of peerless strain.
I have not time
The whole of her long history
To utter to the lyre in dulcet rhyme ;
Lest surfeit coming cause annoy.
But at my feet her freshest gain
Is waiting me, my debt to thee ;
Let this have course on wings my art contrives, my boy.

For pressing on
Thy mother's brothers' path
In wrestle, no disgrace
Thou bring'st to Theognetus, who
Olympia's chaplet won, nor dimm'st the fame
Of Isthmic glories stout Kleitomachus's due :
But, aggrandizing thy Midylian race,
Thou show'st the saying true,
Which erst Oïkleus' son
Spake darkly, when his comrades' children came
To seven-gated Thebes in wrath

From Argos land.
Siege-lines a second time the Afterborn had manned ;
And then he cried,
Whileas he watched the doubtful field,
" There glows in sons their father's native tide
Of stubborn purpose.   Perfectly
My son, my own Alkmaion, stand
Wielding, displayed on sanguine shield,
His spotted dragon next to Kadmus' gates I see.

And he who bore   ·
Defeat and loss in that ill-omened siege of yore,
The hero-king
Adrastus, now the message meets
Of less unlucky birds, though sorrowing
Shall fill his home.   For only he
Of all the Danaan host once more
Shall come to Abas' spacious streets
With all his people safe, for so the gods decree,

Bearing along
The melancholy way
The bones of his dead son."
So spake Amphiaraüs.   I

Myself Alkmaion joy with wreaths t' adorn,
Sprinkling his tomb with copious song.   For he anigh
  My homestead dwells, and all that I have won
      He guards, and passing by,
      When to the theme of song
  Earth's centre-spot I went, his art inborn
    Of prophecy he put in play.

    And thou, O god
Whose arrows fly afar, whose glorious abode
      In Pytho's dells
  All comers welcomes, thought'st it meet
There to confer the prize that all excels.
    And in his island home before
    Thou at thy feast hast once bestowed
    The envied name of pentathlete
On him.   And now, O king, with kindness, I implore

    Thee, look upon
The skein of song I weave, each feat that he has done
      To celebrate.
    Beside the vocal revelry
  Calm Justice stood : and I for your estate
    Xenarkes, would of heaven entreat

Regard undying.   Since if one
Without exceeding toil should be
Successful, to the crowd of fools he haps to meet

He seems by lore
And wise contrivances
With Fortune's gifts to crown
His life.   Yet this is not in man :
'Tis God that grants them : who will one upraise
To-day, another lift to-morrow, as he can
Sink others 'neath their power's level down.
But thou on Megaran
And Marathonian shore
Hast won, and thrice thy native Hera's bays
In combat, Aristomenes.

Four times beneath
Thy body thrown thy rivals felt thy ruthless breath
Above them burn.
And not to them alike and thee
In Pytho was decreed a glad return :
Nor, when they reached their mother's roof,
Did laughter sweet of greeting kith
Wait them ; but sore with misery

They skulk in devious lanes from foemen's jeers aloof.

But if it chance
That fresh good fortune fall a mortal's lot to hance
In tender age,
Aloft on wings of mighty hope
He soars in manhood's struggles to engage
With nobler aim than rich to be.
For, mortals' pleasure to advance,
A little luck gives ample scope ;
As fast it falls to earth, shaken by stern decree.

Things of a day !
What is our somebody ?
And what our cipher ?   Here
Man is the vision of a shade :
But when the ray that Zeus bestows has shone,
His light at once is clear, his life is easy made.
In freedom's road, Aigina, mother dear,
With Zeus' and Peleus' aid
Conduct this city aye,
With royal Aiakus, good Telamon,
And with Achilles' bravery !

9. To Telesikrates of Kyrene.

THE man who armed with shield of brass has won
 The prize of Pytho's ring
With the deep-bosomed Graces fain am I to sing;
 Brave Telesikrates exceeding blest
  Styling, the crown
Of fair Kyrene's chariot-driving town.
 Her Leto's son with flowing hair
From Pelion's wind-haunted valleys bare
Away long since; and brought on car of gold
The huntress maid to Libya, and possessed
 Of lands that teem with grain and sheep;
The third full share of branching earth to keep
  For ever in her hold,
   The fairest e'er
 A blooming mistress gazed upon.

And silver-footed Aphrodite there

Her guest from Delos' isle
Made welcome, as she touched with dainty hand the while
  The god-built chariot ; and a lovely veil
     In kindness spread
  Of modesty around their nuptial bed ;
   And yoked the god in wedlock's bands
With Hypseus' child ; Hypseus', who o'er broad lands
Of daring Lapithæ was then the king :
The second from Okeänus in male
  Descent ; whom, gladdened by the love
Peneius proffered her, where towering
   His famous vales above
    Mount Pindus stands,
  The water-nymph Kreüsa bare,

Daughter of Gaia.   Her her father bred
A maiden fair of arm, Kyrene clept :
Who loved not to and fro before the loom to tread,
   Nor cared at all
   To hold gay festival
With girl-companions who at home were kept.
  But, armed with brazen dart and sword,
   She waged a deadly strife
With beasts of prey ; and through her constant ward

Her father's herds enjoyed a long and peaceful life.
　　　Or, if she slept,
　　Scant courtesy she stayed to show
　　To slumber, though the sweetest bedfellow,
If up the eastern sky the day to dawning crept.

　　And thus it chanced Apollo one fair morn
　　　Surprised her all alone
In struggle weaponless against a lion grown.
　　Then straight the ample-quivered Archer-god
　　　With rousing cry
　　Old Cheiron summoned from his home hard by:
　　"Come out, O son of Philyre,
　　From yonder solemn cave; in ecstasy　　　　•
　　The spirit and the wondrous force behold
　　That clothe at times a maiden's womanhood!
　　　See how upon her dauntless head
　　She brings the strife, for labour overbold,
　　　With soul unmoved by dread!
　　　　Whose child is she?
　　From what firm stock has she been torn

　　The hollows of the dusky hills to keep?
　　　Behold how infinite

The prowess she delights in ! Tell me, were it right
   At once by strength of hand to make her mine ?
      Or better, wed
  To cull the honied harvest of her bed ? "
   To him the Kentaur all aglow,—
While lightly laughter lit his kindly brow,—
With counsel deep advising straight replied.
" Persuasion hides the keys of love divine ;
   And wise, O Phoibos, is her way :
And laws of gods and men alike decide
    'Tis shame in open day,
      As thou must know,
  A maiden's virgin flower to reap.

Nay but a soft impulse has prompted thee,
  Who mayst not, if thou would'st, have aught to do
With falsehood, thus to speak in insincerity.
    Dost thou require
     O king, to ask the sire
Of yonder maiden ? Thou ! the prophet who
  Hast knowledge of th' appointed end
    Of all things, and the course
  They follow ? All the leaves that earth will send
To deck the spring-time, all the sands that 'neath the force

Of waves or wind
In sea or river whirl, and how
And what shall be the future thou dost know.
But if I must with thee be measured mind for mind,

I tell thee to this valley thou art come
With spells upon thee laid
To wed and o'er the sea to bear this very maid
To Zeus's peerless garden, sovereign
To make her there ;
Gathering an island people to repair
To her plain-girdled hill : yea now
Thy noble bride in homes with gold that glow
Will queenly Libya, rich in spreading lea,
Receive for thee with gladness ; there her plain
At once will share with her, to own
In common with herself, in loyalty ;
Where all the fruit-trees known
In plenty grow,
And beasts of prey the forest roam.

There she shall bear a son, whom instantly
Illustrious Hermes shall
To Gaia carry and the thronèd Hours withal

Straight from his loving mother's breast ; and they
    The baby, set
Up on their knees, with constant drops shall pet
  Of nectar and ambrosia's dew ;
And make as though he were immortal too,
A Zeus, or Phoibos all immaculate,
A present source of joy to friends alway :
  Whom some as Shepherd, Huntsman, Herd,
As Aristaius some, shall celebrate."
    And so with many a word
      He urged the two
  To end their bridal speedily.

Short is the road, and quickly perfected
The deed, when gods would hasten.   That same day
Beheld the work complete.   In Libya's golden bed
    The loving pair
  Were joined in wedlock ; where
She rules a city lovely till to-day
  And famous for her victories.
    And now in Pytho's game
Divine the son of staunch Karneiades
Has blent the wreath that crowns good fortune with her name,
    When conquering

He shouted out "Kyrene."   She
Will gladly welcome one who brings in glee
To her fair-womened land the prize of Delphi's ring.

To mighty excellences aye belong
    Of right protracted tales :
But lengthy themes to paint with brevity avails
  To win a wise man's hearing.   After all
      All issues be
Betwixt the hands of Opportunity.
  Whom Iolaüs long ago,
As seven-gated Thebes has cause to know,
Held not dishonoured.   Him, when he had made
Eurystheus' head before his falchion fall,
  She buried where Amphitryon
The charioteer beneath the sod was laid,
    His grandsire, 'mongst the Sown
      Who used to go,
  Where milkwhite steeds the roadway throng,

A welcome guest erewhile in Kadmus' town.
  Embraced by him and Zeus,
One travail abled wise Alkmena to produce
  Twin sons with strength to win in battle.   He

Who could not sing
Of Herakles, who e'er could Dirke's spring,
  That nurtured him and Iphikles,
Forget, were dumb. To them for kindnesses
Received, and prayers accomplished I my lay
Will carol. O ye vocal Graces, still
  Let the unsullied light ye shed
Not quit me. In Aigina's isle, I say,
    And thrice on Nisus' hill,
      This man on this
    His state has heaped immense renown,

By action 'scaping silent helplessness.
So, be his townsman friend or enemy,
How well he has for all endured the struggle's stress
      Let no man hide ;
    But loyally abide
The maxim of the Old Man of the Sea ;
  Who said that e'en a foe should praise
    His fellowman with all
His heart who got him fame by honest ways.
Full oft they saw at Pallas' stated festival
    Thee win, when dame
    And maid, though nought they spoke aloud,

L

Each to herself a longing sweet avowed
Thee, Telesikrates, for son or spouse to claim :

So in the feast of Zeus Olympian,
    And ample-bosomed Ge,
And all thy country's games, it thus fell out.   And me
  The ancient glory of thy long descent
      Compels again,
  Though slaked my thirst for song, to raise the strain,
    And hymn the suitors brave and good,
  Who gathered for a maid of Libyan blood
  To Irasa, Antaius' child to wed,
  Famed for the beauty of her locks, intent.
    And many a kindred chieftain came
  To ask her hand, and many a stranger too ;
      For not by glozing fame
        Was she endued
    With beauty's gifts ; and every man

  The fruiting blossom of her golden grace
    Of youth was fain to cull.
But for his child her sire conceived a match more full
  Of honour. He had heard how Danaüs,
      Of Argos' state

The lord, for daughters twice a score and eight
　One morning ere the full noonday
Provided speedy mates.　In long array
Beyond the goal the whole fair sisterhood
He set at once, and bade the numerous
　Aspirants to a sonship's tie
Before him in the course by fortitude
　　And speed in running try
　　　Which daughter they
　Should get according to their pace.

And so the Libyan king a bridegroom gave
His daughter : by the goal he bade her stand,
The struggle's prime reward, in garments rich and brave,
　　And cried aloud
　　To all the eager crowd
That whosoe'er should soonest lay his hand
　Upon her robes the girl should gain.
　　Alexidamus then,
For fast his footsteps fled across the plain,
Caught hand in hand the prize he loved and 'mongst his men
　　In triumph led ;
　And glad his nomad horsemen threw
　A storm of leaves on him and garlands too ;
For oft before Success had lighted on his head.

10. To Hippokleas of Thessaly.

Oh ! happy Sparta ! blessèd Thessaly !
    For either land
    One father's progeny,
The sons of Herakles the lord of war, command.
    Why boast I thus untimely ? Nay
    But Pytho and Pelinna call on me,
    And chiefs who grace Aleuas' pedigree,
    Hippokleäs' success to sing,
    With them who now in triumph bring
The victor home, in laudatory lay.

For now he tastes the sweets of victory,
    Whom to the crowd
    Of neighbour peasantry
Parnassus' inmost vale has just proclaimed aloud
    The foremost of the boyish quire
    Who ran the double course. O Phoibos, sweet

Is goal and start to men who hap to meet
A god to spur them on.   And thou
Hast planned his latest conquest now,
Who follows in the footsteps of his sire

With bent hereditary.   Twice arrayed
In Ares' warlike panoply
He carried off Olympia's victory :
Aye and the contest in the mead
'Neath Kirrha's rock has made
The name of Phrikias renowned for speed.
And so in days to come
May Fate bid high success for them to bloom ;

And—which in Hellas is a gift most rare—
Let them be free
From what we mortals share,
Reverses from a god's offended jealousy !
A god alone is griefless aye ;
But he must be esteemed a happy man,
And one that bards should celebrate, who can
Through excellence of hand or foot
By strength and daring resolute
The most desired of prizes bear away ;

And still alive behold a youthful son
      Formally crowned
    With wreaths at Pytho won.
The brazen heavens are still to him forbidden ground;
     But every joy of every kind,
    That we of mortal race delight in, lies
Within his reach : no further now he plies
     His oars.   Thou'lt nor by sea nor land
     Find the strange pathway to the band
Of them that live beyond the Northern Wind.

Yet with them princely Perseus carnival
     Held merrily in days of old,
When, hecatombs of asses manifold
     While to the god they slew, he stepped
     By hap within their hall;
Whose rites and hymns Apollo's self have kept
     In laughter, 'mid the feast
To see the rampant pranks of every beast.

And yet the Muse to such outlandish ways
     Doth not refuse
    Her presence. Maidens' lays
And spirit-stirring lyres and shrilly pipes they use

For cheer, and garlanding their hair
With woven coronals of golden bays,
They pass in jocund revel all their days.
Nor carking care nor fell disease
Disturbs their calm divinities ;
But rid of battle's toil and labour's care

They dwell from Retribution's cruel ire
Entirely free.
And thither with the fire
Of valiance in his heart the son of Danaë—
For guide Athena with him went—
Came, to the hidden mansions of the crew
Of happy folk : and he the Gorgon slew,
And bore that head which serpents wreathe
In mottled braids, a stony death,
Home to his islanders.   Not mine the bent,

Whate'er the gods may work, to scant belief,
Or marvel at their might.
Let go the oars : the bower anchor tight,
Quick as thou canst, in earth imbed ;
Ere on some hog's-back reef
Thou strike and founder.   For my Muse has fled,

Like flitting honey-bee,
Elsewhere to quaff her draughts of poesy.

And hope I have that while in Ephyre
    Her people pour
    My dulcet minstrelsy
From triumph-gladdened throats along Peneius' shore,
    For sake of laurels he has worn
I may some day to elder men and young
Hippokleäs' deserts in worthier song
    Make glorious, the maiden's theme
    Of waking thought and sleeping dream.
    By loves diverse are divers spirits torn ;

But if what any seek with eager quest
    He hap to win,
    The prize he has possessed,
So sorely longed for, let him take his pleasure in :
    For what within a year may be
Nor sign nor token can foreshadow.   I
On Thorax' kindly friendliness rely,
    Who toiled to harness, me to please,
    This car of the Pierides
With mutual love and mutual instancy.

It needs the Lydian stone of proof to try
    Gold and a soul upright.
So to his brothers brave will I indite
   My praise, because the olden fame
    Of Thessaly on high
Their excellence exalts. 'Tis aye the same :
    In men of right intent
Lies only wise paternal government.

11. To Thrasydaius of Thebes.

DAUGHTER of Kadmus, Semele,
Who to Olympus' courts a guest art come ;
And Ino, goddess white, who in the sea
  Hast with the Nereids thy home ;
With Herakles' illustrious mother haste,
    To Melia's shrine repair,
    The golden tripod's treasury
    That none may tread, with honour rare
      That Loxias has graced,

The truthful seat of prophecies
For his Ismenius named.   For now he calls
The host of country demigoddesses
  Who dwell around within her walls
To meet ; while ye, whom sweet Harmonia bore,
    Shall holy Themis hymn
    And Pytho, and the just decrees

Of earth's mid stone, when faint and dim
   The twilight is no more,

Our seven-gated Thebes to laud, and Kirrha's quest ;
   Where Thrasydaius brought
To mind the hearth by which his fathers knelt,
Crowned with the third glad crown for triumph wrought
In Pylades' rich corn-fields, where a guest
Orestes, fled from Lakedaimon, dwelt.

   Him, when his father met his death,
From Klytemnestra's hands Arsinoë
His nurse, who dreaded force or lack of faith
   With mournful issue, took, when she
Kassandra, Priam's daughter Trojan-bred,
   With cold gray steel beside
Her husband Agamemnon's wraith
Despatched along the shady side
   Of Acheron to tread.

   The ruthless woman ! Was it, pray,
Iphigeneia by Euripus' strait
Slain as a victim far from home away
   Provoked her heavy-handed hate ?

Or did the pleasures of a stranger's bed
   Lead her astray ? a crime
  Esteemed in youthful brides alway
  Most hateful, one for length of time
    That ne'er is coverèd

By stranger tongues ; for folk delight in slanderous speech.
    And when success is great
  No lesser envy it encounters ; he
  Unseen may fret who keeps a low estate.
  So Atreus' hero-son just lived to reach
  Farfamed Amyklæ, when by treachery

   He perished, and the prophet-maid
  Whelmed in destruction, who her Troy had burned ;—
  Its homes for Helen's sake in ruin laid,
   Its splendour all to ashes turned.
  To aged Strophius then for guestship came
   The youngster, who beneath
   Parnassus dwelt ; till Ares' aid
  Helped him at last to put to death
   Aigisthus and his dame.

  My friends, I fancy that to-day,

Though I have trod the path direct before,
Some labyrinth has led my steps astray ;
  Or, like a boat from sight of shore,
Far from my course the breezes me have borne.
    But thine the task, my Muse,
    If thou hast underta'en for pay
    To sing thy hireling song, to choose
      Themes fitter to adorn

Young Thrasydaius here, or else his sire who won
      The Pythian wreath of eld.
  The kindliness and honour of their race
Shine as the sun : for long ago they held,
Where far-renowned Olympia's course is run
By swiftest steeds, the victor's splendid place ;

    And where unclad the rivals start
To run afoot, all Hellas' host for speed
  They shamed at Pytho. Should the gods impart
    Distinction, I were fain indeed
To clasp whate'er in each succeeding age
      I could : but when I see
    That citizens of modest heart
    Live happy longest, royalty

I reckon sorry wage.

For common ends my bow is bent
T' achieve success.   The ruin Envy wreaks
Is foiled, if he who wins the height, content
In quiet his enjoyment seeks,
And bids offensive insolence begone.
He better at the last
Will meet black Death, his monument
The best, a name that nought shall blast,
But children joy to own.

'Tis this that Iölaüs son of Iphikles,
The theme of many a song,
Distinguishes, and thee, of seed divine,
King Polydeukes, and thy Kastor strong,
Who days alternate sleep in Therapne's
Dark tomb, alternate in Olympus shine.

12. To Midas of Akragas.

I PRAY thee, spendour-loving queen,
Most beauteous city known to mortal ken,
　　Seat of Persephone,
Who on the sheep-fed banks of Akragas
Inhabitest a hill where goodly mansions rise,
　　　　Benignantly
Receive with kind assent of gods and men
For noble Midas this his Pythian wreath ;
　　And eke himself, who has
　　Victorious over Hellas been
　　In that sweet art which great
Pallas Athena first produced, wherewith
　　　　To imitate
With skill the savage Gorgons' lamentable cries.

　　Which sadly flowing forth she heard
From those two spinster throats in weary woe,

And many a serpent-head
That none can near, when Perseus' steel had slain
The third who with them shared their dismal sisterhood :
Before he sped
Home to his sea-girt isle, a fatal foe
To all Scriphus' folk.   From Phorkus' seed
Divine their sight was ta'en ;
And gruesome was his gift conferred
On Polydektes, through
The bridal forced and serfdom's cleaving need
The mother knew
Who bore him, when fair-cheeked Medusa's head was viewed

The prize of him whom Danaë
Brought forth, the son according to repute
Of gold's spontaneous shower.
But when from these his toils the hero whom
She loved she had preserved, the virgin-goddess wrought
The changeful power
Of varied music, bass and treble flute,
To counterfeit with instruments the groan
Of pain that issued from
The jaws of keen Euryale.
She made it, and to men

Gave it, the 'air of many-headed tone'
By name, since when
It minds men of the games by thronging thousands sought ;

Breathing its notes through metal thin
And reeds, that nigh the Graces' city grow
Within Kephisis' grove,
Where well the dance is led, true witnesses
To them that measures tread.   If any happiness
We men may prove,
Not free from toil it shows itself ; yet so
Fortune perhaps will perfect it to-day ;
But whatso fated is
No man at all can fail to win.
For that good time shall be,
When, though he seem a helpless castaway,
Prosperity
With unexpected luck, the pledge of more, will bless.

ISTHMIAN ODES.

1. To Herodotus of Thebes.

My mother, golden-shielded Thebes, thy fame
Of higher count than all my business shall be.
Yet be not wroth with me, thou rugged Delian isle,
    For whom my soul in minstrelsy
  Has spent herself. To folk of honest name
What can be dearer than their sires? Give place awhile,
Thou land of Phoibos! Both, with heaven to succour me,

  Will I in common honours blend; and sweet
Unshorn Apollo with her sturdy seamen sing
In foam-girt Keos; ay and Isthmus' ridge that fends
    Salt water; since 'twas his to bring
  Six crowns from where the rivals brave compete
To Kadmus' warrior sons for conquest that commends
My native land, wherein her son unwavering

    Alkmena bore;

Whose step the angry hounds of Geryon quailed before.
  And fain would I exalt Herodotus
      In music's strains,
  Who with four steeds has proved victorious,
    Letting no other hold the reins :
      Wherefore in song
  With Iolaüs or with Kastor strong
    I fain would couple him ; for they,
  In Thebes and Sparta born in th' olden day,
Were best of charioteers the hero-host among ;

  And in the festive lists most frequently
Contended for the prize, and decked with tripods rare
Their homes, and caldrons too and bowls of massive gold ;
    While garlands gleaming in their hair
  Gave them to taste the sweets of victory ;
And clear their prowess shines whom all could then behold
Full-armed with clanging shield as oft as running bare.

  How well those hands would cast th' unerring spear,
Or send the quoit of stone aloft the sky to rend !
For no man then had heard the name of ' pentathlete,'
    But every bout its proper end
  Achieved : and these would garlanded appear

Full oft with wreath on wreath by Dirke's waters sweet,
Or where the streams of proud Eurotas sea-ward wend ;

      He who could own
For father Iphikles, compatriot of the Sown ;
   The son of Tyndareus th' Achaian height
      Of Therapne
Inhabiting. I greet ye, men of might !
   But now I trim my melody
      Isthmus divine,
Onchestus' shingles, and Poseidon's shrine
   To praise ; and so will celebrate
In this man's victory the glorious fate
That waits upon his sire Asopodorus' line,

And his adopted home Orchomenus,
That gave him shelter, when in seas without a shore,
Hard pressed by shipwreck, all the frost he knew
   Of evil hap. But now once more
  The old congenial tide of prosperous
Good fortune flows again : and one that has gone through
Distress, thereafter sets by prudence hearty store.

   But if a man his every effort use,

Nor spare expenditure nor toil, renown to gain,
'Tis due to them that find it with ungrudging heart
　　To bring the proud, exultant, strain ;
　For light the recompense of poet's Muse
For hardships manifold, although the song impart
A public monument that aye shall fair remain.

　　　For, whatsoe'er
It be, the wage is sweet that guerdons human care :
　And shepherd, farmer, fowler, he who feeds
　　　Upon the sea,
　Have one intent, to satisfy the needs
　　Of hunger crying ceaselessly.
　　　But when for game
　Or battle nobly won their loud acclaim
　　Both countrymen and strangers pour
　With one consent to hail the conqueror,
His is the highest meed, the very flower of fame.

　But stay ! 't is time to change the theme, and bless
Our neighbour Kronos-born, the Shaker of the Earth,
Inventor of the car and patron of the horse ;
　　And those to thee who trace their birth,
　Amphitryon ; and Minyas' recess ;

Demeter's storied grove Eleusis, and the course
That gently trends beside Euboia's winding firth.

I add thy own and thy Achaian's shrine,
Protesilaüs, in Thessalian Phylake.
But every spot to name, where on Herodotus
    Presiding Hermes victory
  Conferred for harnessed steeds, this lay of mine
Would still be all too short though ne'er so copious :
And reticence is oft the best of flattery.

    Be it his fate
On shining wings of sweet Pierian maids elate
 ' To soar, and yet in Pytho's vale, and where
    Alpheius flows
Beside Olympia's course, with garlands fair—
  The choicest wreaths that Hellas knows—
    To fill his hand ;
Building fresh honour for his native land,
  Thebes of the seven gates. But when
One hoards hid wealth and jeers at fellow men,
Thoughtless he dooms his soul unsung to Hades' strand.

2. To Thrasyboulus of Akragas.

Oft, Thrasyboulus, in the ancient days
The bards who on the stately car could climb
   Where sit the Muses, golden bays
   About their brows, in lightsome rhyme
Clasping their honoured lyres would deftly aim
Their honied song to glorify the boys
Whose ripe young beauty set their hearts aflame
   For regal Aphrodite's joys.

For in those days not yet had Poesy
Grown avaricious, nor for hire would slave ;
   Not then did sweet Terpsichore
   For coin let any bidder have
The dulcet music of her gentle tones
All lacquered o'er with silver.   Now forsooth
She bids us bear in mind the Argive's groans,
   Not so far off the path of Truth.

"'T is money, money, money makes the man,"
  Reft of his goods and friends at once, he cried.
But, for thyself art wise, a triumph not unknown
  I hymn, which, where competing horses ran
  At Isthmus, to Xenokrates alone
    Poseidon gave, the crown to own
  Of Doric parsley round his tresses tied,

Gracing a clever charioteer, the light
  Of all in Akragas. In Krisa fair,
    Viewed by Apollo vast of might,
    He carried off his laurels there ;
  And honoured by Erechtheus' noble kin
  In olive-dowered Athens, spake not ill
  Of him who neatly whipped his chariot in
    With all a driver's handy skill,

Nikomachus, who saw the time to loose
  His every rein; whom all the heralds knew,—
    Proclaimers of the sacred truce
    Of Kronian Zeus in Elis,—who
  Had erst enjoyed his hospitality,
  And greeted him with softest melody
  Of gratulating song, when at the knee

He fell of golden Victory

In that their own dear land, which mortals call
The precinct of Olympian Zeus, wherein
Ainesidamus' sons an immortality
   Of fame achieved. For in thy father's hall,
  O Thrasyboulus, joyful revelry,
    Mingled with honied poesy,
Has oft upraised its glad accustomed din.

No rugged rock nor weary uphill road
Have they to climb, who music's honours bring
   To honourable men's abode
   From them that dwell beside the spring
Of Helikon. Oh! would to heaven that these
My quoits might so far distance other men's,
As all in kindly ways Xenokrates
   Excelled. Amidst his citizens

His carriage was most reverend, and aye
His stables after Panhellenic law
   He kept, and each god's holiday
   Made welcome. Ne'er did sudden flaw
Of tempest make him shorten sail around

His hospitable table, evermore
In summer's heat to cooling Phasis bound,
   In winter's cold to Nile's hot shore.

Let him not now, because about the heart
Of mortals jealous thoughts delight to cling,
Dead silence keep about his father's excellence,
   Nor these my songs.   To play no idle part
   I fashioned them.   So when thou comest hence
     To his, my honoured friend's, presence
Thus, Nikasippus, pay thy welcoming.

3. To Melissus of Thebes.

If any man by glorious feats of strength,
 Or store of honest gold, have got him fame,
Yet curbs within his soul besetting insolence,
 He well deserves that on his name
His countrymen should heap their praises. Excellence,
 O Zeus, to mortals comes of thee :
 And reverential folk prosperity
 Have more enduring than their neighbourhood ;
 While crooked hearts their seeming good,
Though flourishing awhile, will leave alone at length.

For noble deeds beholders it behoves
 To recompense the brave with noble song,
And kindly him to laud who leads the gay parade.
 Now to Melissus here belong
Twin crowns for conquests twain : the one in Isthmus' glade
 By favourable Fate was sent

To turn his heart to jocund merriment ;
The other gathered in the hollow glen
    Of the deep-chested lion. when
He bade them shout the name of Thebes, the Thebes he loves,

    Where rival chariots ran, victorious.
        Nor does he put to shame
    Th' hereditary courage of his kin.
        Ye well have known
        How oft Kleonymus
    The honours of the chariot-race would win :
And so his mother's folk, who trace to Labdakus
        Their pedigree,
Gat wealth by four-in-hands.   But rollingly
        Time plays a changing game.
    The sons of gods from hurt are free alone.

4. To Melissus of Thebes.

THANKS to the gods ten thousand paths are mine,
 In all directions stretched, to tell in song,—
Since thou at Isthmus hast thy ready skill displayed,—
 The virtues which their whole life long,
E'en to its final close, have decked by heavenly aid
 The children of Kleonymus.
 But oft, Melissus, will the boisterous
 Storm-wind on mortals with resistless fórce
 Swoop down, and drive them from their course
This way and that, like ships across the brine.

 However from the first beginning these
 In Thebes, men say, were honourable held,
And all the neighbourhood with hospitality
 Entreated ; yet the promptings quelled
Of full-mouthed arrogance.   Whate'er the eulogy
 Of boundless glory gossipèd

From mouth to mouth of men about their dead
Or living fellows, they no lesser fame
    Attained : for manly deeds their name
Has reached land's farthest end, the posts of Herakles.

For further worth to strive may nought avail.
    Horse-breeders they became,
And favour gat with Ares brazen-clad ;
        But in one day
    The savage, stormy, hail
Of warfare robbed their hearth so lately glad
Of four good men at once.   Yet now the weary tale
        Of wintry gloom
And fitful months is past, and earth in bloom
    With spring of fresh-won fame,
As if with crimson roses, strews their way

By ordinance of gods.   And he who smites
The earth, inhabiting Onchestus' fane
And yon sea-bridge that lies before Korinthus' walls,
    Inspiring this my wondrous strain,
To life the old Renown of noble deeds recalls
    Done by the family, long lain
    Asleep on Lethe's bed ; but now again,

N

Waked out of that dead slumber, she is seen
    Bright bodily with fairest sheen,
As Morning-star among the welkin's lesser lights.

    She in the meads of Athens heralded
    His chariot's victory, at Sikyon
With sprays of song, like these I weave, from them that chose
    To woo the Muses long agone
In the Adrasteän lists his triumph o'er his foes
    She hailed.   Nor kept they e'er afar
    From common gatherings their bended car;
    But joyed with Panhellenic company
    In lavish horsemanship to vie.
In nameless silence they who venture naught are dead;

    And even them that fight obscurity
    Will often ill requite,
Before they reach the long projected height.
    For like event
    Not aye impartially
Does luck bestow; and men of greater might
The craft of lesser folk o'ertaking suddenly
    Will overthrow.
The tale of Aias' bloody feat ye know;

And how he fell that night
On his own sword : to Hellas' sons who went

To Troy a sore reproach.   Yet in his day
Did Homer honour him o'er other men ;
Who all his prowess told in song divinely sweet
Of measured cadence, which since then
Our after generations o'er and o'er repeat.
For so far immortality
Waits on the gift of real poesy,
That if a bard have uttered words of worth,
O'er all the sea and fruitful earth
For ever goes unquenched good work's refulgent ray.

Be ours the Muses' kindly-minded hour,
To kindle that undying torch of song
E'en for Melissus here, of old Telesias
The seed ; a crown to suit the strong
In box and wrestle both.   For he in spirit was,
And courage high, and tireless toil,
A match for lions roaring for their spoil ;
Cunning as vixen on her back that lies
And all the eagle's swoops defies :
For need 't was anywise to foil his foeman's power.

For not to him Orion's mighty thews
  Had kindly nature given ;
To look upon he seemed contemptible ;
    But for a fall
    'Twere difficult to choose
One heavier to throw.   And thus they tell
How once from Kadmus' Thebes to swart Antaius' cell
    In Libya grown
With wheat, where he Poseidon's fane would crown
    With scalps from strangers riven,
There came Alkmena's son, of stature small

But soul unbending, vowed to overawe
His violence by force and make it cease.
He to Olympus went, when all the earth, and all
    The cliffs that fence the hoary seas,
He had explored, and smoothed a passage safe withal
    For voyagers ; and for reward
  In bliss supreme beside the Aigis-lord
  He dwells, esteemed by all the gods beside
    A friend, with Hebe for his bride,
Monarch of golden halls, and Hera's son-in-law.

Wherefore for him above the Amber-gate

Do we his countrymen the feast prepare,
Making with wreaths of flowers new-cut his altars gay,
    And burn our sacrifices there
To those dead sons of his, the eight whom Megara,
    The child of Kreon, bore for him,
    And iron slaughtered. Soon as day is dim,
    With set of sun for them another light
    Arising shines throughout the night,
Lashing the lurid air with smoke of burning fat :

    Till with the second day the yearly game
        A fitting ending has
    In trial of strong muscles : where this man
        A second time
        His wreath of conquests wear
We saw, his brow with myrtle-flowers wan.
A third he gained before in boyhood, giving ear
        To counsels sage
Of him who trained and steered his tender age.
        Wherefore with Orseäs
    Him will I celebrate in joyful rhyme.

5. To Phylakides of Aigina.

O THEIA, worshipped under many names,
Mother of Helios, for thy regard
Man reckons gold above all things beside
In mighty strength : for thee on ocean wide
Ship vies with ship, and horses in the games
Their chariots drag at speed for thy award,
Where in the circles swift of contest they are seen
    To court thy glance, immortal Queen.

And he in that contested struggle gains
An honour all the world would fain acquire,
Around whose tresses many garlands meet
For skilful hands or swiftness of his feet.
But heaven alone to mortal man ordains
Prowess : and two endowments must conspire
To blend their nurturing, ere life's sweet flower can come
    In happiness to perfect bloom ;

Success in act the first, the second fair

Repute.   Yet deem not in thy folly thou canst pair

      With Zeus.   If this

      The highest hap

That men attain be dropped upon thy lap,

Thou hast enough : for mortal blessings are

Befitting mortals.   Thee, Phylakides,

Isthmus and Nemeä crowned in double list ;

    And Pytheäs was pancratist.

My heart no relish has for song th' Aiakidæ's

Renown that mentions not ; and with my melodies

    And Lampo's sons to this well-ordered town

I now am come.   Grudge not to one devote

To walk the stainless paths of deeds divine

The song with seemly boasting to combine

For ended toil.   For in the days long flown

The goodly warriors of heroic note

Gat gain of minstrels' tales ; whose glories citterns tell,

    And many-voicèd oboes swell

    Their fame for countless years.   Their excellence

For poets' song provides material,

Since Zeus so wills ; and bardic carols rise

At every bright Aitolian sacrifice
To Oineus' sons ; at Thebes her citizens
Laud Iolaüs ; Argos' festival
Perseus exalts ; while Polydeukes is the theme,
    And Kastor, by Eurotas' stream :

But in Oinone all the legend runs
Of genial Aiakus and his great-hearted sons ;
      Who twice the ranks
      Of battle led
To sack the Trojans' city, marshallèd
Once by Alkeides, by th' Atreidæ once.
Now quit the plain, and higher soar, and say
By whom did Kyknus fall, and Hektor?   Who
    The fearless mailclad Memnon slew,
Swart Aithiopia's chief?   Whose shaft amidst the fray
Smote goodly Telephus beside Kaïkus banks ?

Heroes for whom Aigina's peerless shore
I claim for mother-land.   Long since was built
Her tower for high-exalted excellence
To mount.   And many shafts of eloquence
My ready tongue has in redundant store,
To loose in praise of them : and thou too wilt,

Fair Salamis, the town of Aias, testify
   How in the war not long gone by

  Her sailors saved thee from the smiting storm,
  When human life-blood showered thick as hail
  From countless slain. Yet quench the pæan now
  In silence. Zeus alone can good bestow
  And evil, Zeus, of schemes that mortals form
  Supreme disposer. In the rhymer's tale
Honours like these delight reward as honey sweet
    To harvest. Let who will compete,

  That knows the fame of Kleonikus' race,
By deeds from them to win the athlete's foremost place.
     The mighty moil
     That they endure
  Goes not to waste, nor does th' expenditure
  Expectant hope of crowns to come efface.
  So Pytheäs I praise, whose masterful
  Hands made Phylakides's victory
    Assured ; a deft opponent he !
Then bear him hence a crown, a chaplet of fine wool,
And wingèd song and new withal to grace his toil.

6. To Phylakides of Aigina.

As though at full of festive revelry,
We mix the second cup of Muse-inspirèd song
    For Lampo's offspring strong
      In tireless thews.
    The first in Nemeä we drained
      To thee, O Zeus,
  When there the flower of coronals was gained ;
  And this at Isthmus, Isthmus' lord, to thee,
And Nereus' daughters fair two score and ten, we bring ;
For now Phylakides, his youngest, victory
    Has gotten : be it ours ere long,
    To the Olympian saviour offering,
To bathe Aigina's isle in honied melody !

    For if a man in generous expense
Takes pleasure, and in toil, and aye unflinching meets
      The labours their own feats

Have sanctified,
For him delicious fame the gods
Will plant beside
His path : god-honoured in the inmost roads
Of bliss his barque has anchor cast. Propense
To tastes like these the son of Kleonikus prays
Such joy in hoary eld and Hades may attend
Himself; and towards the lofty seats
Of Klotho and her sister Fates I raise
My voice, to bid them list the wishes of my friend.

And you, ye golden-carred Aiakidæ,
I hold it aye the strictest law to me
To dew with songs of praise, whene'er this isle I reach.
Whose mighty deeds have made them straight and wide
Ten thousand paths, beyond the fountain-head
Of Neilus' fruitful tide,
Beyond the homes of them that dwell behind
The northern wind : nor wilt thou find
A country so uncouth, so gibbering in speech,
As not to be acquaint in some degree
With Peleus' heroism, whose luck it was to wed

The daughter of a god ; nor to have heard

The fame of Aias and his father Telamon.
　　Whom erst Alkmena's son
　　　　In ships led o'er
　　The sea to Troy with Tiryns' might,
　　　　The brazen war
　'To join, a glad ally; to worst in fight
Heroes untold; because his plighted word
Laomedon forswore.　The height of Pergamus
He took; with him he slew the tribes of Meropes;
　　And nigh to Phlegræ lighting on
　Alkyoneus the herdsman mountainous
In girth, his twanging string with hands full merciless

　Alkeides drew.　When Telamon he bade
Come o'er the sea with him, his folk in general
　　　Were keeping festival :
　　　And Telamon—
　Whilst he stood in the lion's skin—
　　　Implored the son
Of bold Amphitryon mighty-speared begin
　By offerings of nectar duly made :
And therewithal the chief a winecup rough with gold
Tendered.　Then he to heaven his hands unconquered spread
　　And thus besought.　" If thou at all,

O Zeus my father, in the days of old
With willing soul to prayer of mine hast listenèd,

    Now, now with most intent request I pray,
    Grant Telamon that he, my guest to-day,
From Eriboia's womb the brave son fore-ordained
    May get ; and let him in his body be
    Impervious to wounds, (as roundabout
        This hide enfoldeth me
    Of that wild beast that erst in Nemeä's dell,
      The first fruits of my labours, fell,)
With dauntless soul to match." He spake; and Zeus unchained
    And sent his eagle, king of birds. Straightway
Sweet gladness woke within his bosom. With a shout

    In prophet-guise he lift his voice, and cried,
"O Telamon, the son thou cravest shall be thine ;
      And for the bird our eyne
        Beheld appear
      Aias shall he be named, of might
        Immense, the fear
    Of folk that toil the War-god to delight."
    He said, and ceasing sat him down beside
The rest to feast. But all their worthiness were long

To tell.   For Pytheäs, Euthymenes, and chief
    Phylakides, O Muse of mine,
  I come to lead the revels.   Let my song
That tells their honours be in Argive fashion brief.

  Three times the laurels of the pancratist
The noble uncle and his sister's children won
      At Isthmus; oft, where on
        The leafy vale
    Of Nemeä mountains frown, men see
      Their skill prevail.
  They bathe the clan of the Psalychidæ
  I' the Graces' freshest dew.   Oh ! such a list
Of songs they brought to light!   Themistius' house they set
Once more on high; and in this favoured place they dwell:
    Where Lampo long his work has done
    With careful love, and reverences yet
Old Hesiod's saw, and bids his offspring con it well ;

  Clothing his town with honours all his own,
  And love for kindnesses to strangers shown.
What to pursue aware, and what to let go by,
  His tongue he lets not overrun his thought.
  Greatest of athletes seems he in our eyes,

As hones from Naxos brought
To temper steel all other stones excel.
Him will I give from Dirke's well
That water pure to drink, that by the progeny
Of wise Mnemosyne with golden gown
At Kadmus' well-embattled gates was bid to rise.

7. To Strepsiades of Thebes.

WITH which of all the honours that befell
　　Thy land of old didst thou delight
Thy spirit most, O Thebes thrice blessèd?　Was it when
　　Thou gavest birth to curly Dionyse
Demeter's comrade, whom the cymbals' symphonies
　　　Extol? or when at night
　　In golden rain thou saw'st descend to men
　　　The chief of them on high that dwell,

　　To cross Amphitryon's gate and seek his bride,
　　　Whence peerless Herakles was born?
Or in Teiresias' supreme sagacity?
　　Or in the skill by Iolaüs shown
As horseman, or the spears untiring of the Sown?
　　　Or when Adrastus, shorn
　　Of his ten thousand comrades, from the cry
　　　Of fight thou dravest back, to bide

In Argos, where they love the horse? or when
    Thy Doric colony
On Lakedaimon's mountain-spurs was set,
And strong Amyklæ fell before the men
Who boasted Aigeus' blood, thy own true progeny,
    Obeying Pytho's prophecies?
    But fairest fame in wondrous wise
Grown old will fall asleep, and folk forget;

Save that which gains the bloom of poesy,
    Yoked with the indestructible
Torrents of minstrel-lore.   Then raise a revel-song
Of sweetest cadence for Strepsiades:
For he has carried off the five great victories
    At Isthmus, terrible
    In thews, in manly excellence as strong,
    And passing fair withal to see;

And by the purple-tressèd Muses he
    Is made illustrious; and new
Sprays of the tree of fame his namesake uncle's tomb
    He twines to deck, whom armed with brazen targe
Dread Ares slew. But, know thou surely, honours large
    To bravery are due.

And whoso in this storm for love of home
  Repels this rain of blood shall be,

For driving ruin on the hostile host,
    For aye, alive or dead,
The greatest glory of his native town.
  And thou, Diodotus's child, hast lost,—
Imagining thyself in Meleäger's stead,
      Amphiaraüs rivalling
    And Hektor in the fight,—thy spring
Of blooming manhood, bravely having shown

Thy prowess, where amid the van of war
  The bravest bore till hope had fled
The battle's brunt.   A grief too deep for words was then
  My portion : but Poseidon deems it good
The tempest's roar to change to happy quietude.
      And I around my head
  Will garlands fit to sing the first of men.
    Nor grudge me, gods, if thus so far,

Each day's delights pursuing while I may,
    I do my best to live at ease
Until to eld and fate's appointed time I come.

For though our lots unequal be, we all
Alike must die at last; and he his soul who shall
  With distant prospects please,
 Will prove too short to reach the burnished home
  Of gods. As in the olden day

 Wide-wingèd Pegasus threw headlong down
  His lord Bellerophon,
 Who sought to win the palaces of heaven,
 The council-halls of Zeus. But e'en renown,
If got by means unfair, an ending waits upon
  Most bitter. Grant us at our prayer,
  O Loxias of golden hair,
 Thy flowery crown at Pytho's contests given!

8. To Kleandros of Aigina.

Ho! boys, let some one go and call
Kleandros and his fellows; bid them raise
    Beside the shining entrance-hall
    Where Telesarchus dwells,
His sire, the revel-song, the glorious recompense
    Of labours finishèd;
    In payment for his Isthmic victory,
      And for that he
At Nemeä the contest's honours won:
      For whom I too,
    Though vexed at heart, am asked to-day
    The golden Muses' aid to pray.
    For now, from mighty sorrow freed,
Let us not stint our coronals, nor feed
      And pamper grief;
    But, bidding useless woe begone,
    Adapt our tongues to merry lays,

Though pain be new.
For now for our relief
The potent spells
Of some kind god have banished hence
The stone of Tantalus, that o'er our head

Was hung, a hardship sore to bear
For Hellas.   But our fears have fled and ta'en
Away our heavy load of care.
'Tis best for man to be
Intent on present things : for Time is treacherous ;
And swiftly rolls the tide
Of life along : but e'en adversity,
So freedom be
Safe, may be bettered.   Man should cherish aye
Good hope with care.
And he is bounden, who was bred
In Thebes the seven-portallèd
The Graces' fairest wreath to bring
For brave Aigina's special honouring.
For twins there were
Born to Asopus, legends say,
His youngest children, daughters twain ;
And either fair

'To royal Zeus was dear.

The other he

By Dirke's fountain beauteous

O'er a car-loving city bade preside :

But thee to Oinops' isle he bare,

And locked in thy embrace he fell asleep.

And to his sire the Thunderer there

The godlike Aiakus

Thou broughtest forth, of men on earth the trustiest :

Who even gods' dispute

Determined.   Sons of his alike divine,

And all their line

Of warfare-loving children, aye excelled

In following

Woe-working battle's brazen din

With manhood ; yet were sober in

Conduct, and wise of soul.   And this

The Council of the Blessed witnesses.

When sharp debate

Zeus over Thetis' wedding held

'Gainst the bright Monarch of the deep,

Each coveting

The maiden for his mate ;

So beauteous
She was, that love inflamed their breast.
Yet of her bed gat neither suitor boot,

Though both immortals ; when they heard
The oracles of Fate: for in their mid
Unerring Themis spake her word,
"Because it is decreed
That if or Zeus himself, or Zeus's brother, wed
The water-goddess, she
A kingly son and greater shall produce
Than even Zeus,
Who shall a weapon than the thunder-flash
More mighty wield
Or dreadful trident ; pray ye cease
Your quarrel : let the girl in peace
With mortal man in marriage-tie
Be joined, and see her son in combat die,
Her son the peer
Of Ares in the battle's clash,
The swiftness of whose feet shall bid
The levin yield.
To Peleus then, if here
My voice ye heed,

Be this high honour offerèd ;

For, sprung from Aiakus, they say that he

Is godliest of all that grow

On broad Iolkos' plain.   Let messengers

To Cheiron's ageless cavern go

At once without delay ;

Nor twice let Nereus' child the lots of brawlsome mood

Force on our hands ; but when

At night the waxing moon is at her full

Let Peleus pull

Away the girdle of her maidenhood."

Thus pleaded she

Addressing Kronos' offspring.   They

With brows immortal to her say

Nodded assent ; nor fruitless fell

Her words and died, for, as the singers tell,

Their very king

Sped forward for the common good

Fair Thetis' bridal.   Rhapsoders

The bravery

Of young Achilles sing

To our dull day ;

Who vine-clad Mysia steeped in blood,

With dark gore dewing Telephus's plain ;

And bridged the way for Atreus' sons'
Return ; and rescued Helen ; with his spear
   Cutting away the bravest ones
    Of Troy, who for a time
Hindered his marshalling the ranks of bloody war
   Upon their own dear fields,
  Hektor the overdaring in the fight,
    And Memnon's might,
And other chiefs. Achilles showed them all
    The dismal land
  Of dread Persephone, when he,
  Prince of the bold Aiakidæ,
  Displayed his high ancestral pride,
And therewithal Aigina glorified.
    So e'en when slain
  He wanted not for musical
Gifts ; for his pyre and grave anear
    The virgin band
   Of Helikon their strain
    Of dirge sublime
Stood singing : for th' immortals are
Agreed, a hero's soul to death who yields

To give to them to hymn.   And so
'Tis now ; for fast the Muses' chariot speeds
To bid the memory brighter glow
Of sturdy Nikokles
The boxer.   Laud ye him who once in Isthmus' glen
The Doric parsley gained ;
Because with hand that none could 'scape he too
Aye overthrew
All neighbouring folk confounded by his force.
Nor less have shown
His honours through the victor son
His noble uncle got.   Let one
Among his fellows haste to twist
For brave Kleandros, hailed the pancratist,
The slender wreath
Of myrtle.   For Alkathoüs' course,
And Epidaurus' youth, his deeds
With fortune's crown
Have met, and plausive breath.
And meet it is
His praise should come from honest men :
· For not in secret sloth his youth was trained.

NEMEAN AND OTHER ODES.

1. To Chromius of Etna.

THOU blossom fair of famous Syracuse.
Alpheius' holy rest, Ortygia,
    Thou bed of Artemis,
Sister of Delos' isle, in thee I find the source
      Of dulcet song,
That hymns, for sake of Etna's sovereign Zeus,
The mighty praise of tempest-footed horse.
    And Chromius' car at Nemea
    In honour of his victories
Compels my strain to join the plaudits of the throng.

For the foundations by the gods were placed
Of yonder mortal's godlike bravery ;
    And in success there lies
The highest excellence of glory ; and to nurse
      The memory
Of noble deeds that conquest's palm has graced

Delights the Muse.   With splendour then asperse
   The isle that to Persephone
   Olympus' king who rules the skies,
Zeus, gave with solemn nod, of earth's fertility

   The very chiefest flower, Sikelia
Rich in the citadels of wealthy towns, to own.
   And therewithal the son of Kronos gave
       A people brave
   To woo on horseback clash of martial steel,
     Nor yet unused to feel
   The golden olive of Olympia
Twined in their tresses.   Oft my shafts not falsely thrown

   Have hit the mark.   And now I stand within
   The outer portals of a host and friend,
     Singing his handsomeness,
Where for my welcoming the fitting feast is decked.
     For yonder courts
   Have large experience of taking in
   The stranger.   They that foolishly expect
   Good fame by slander's tongue to end,
    But water smoke.   For worthiness
Is divers ways displayed, and in their several sorts

Men all should strive their best straightforwardly.
And strength for work avails, for counsel mind,
 The gift inborn to tell
Future events. And thou, Agesidamus' son,
  Hast both of these
 By nature had to use. No wish have I
 Vast wealth in chambers hid to gloat upon ;
  But, always to my neighbours kind,
  In comfort and good name to dwell.
For Hope is free to all, and comes whene'er she please

 To all the sons of toil. But gladly I,
Waking the ancient tale how high his virtue rose,
 Hold fast to Herakles's memory ;
   And sing how he
 The son of Zeus,—from out his mother's womb
  As soon as he had come
 To the fair shining of his father's sky,
With his twin brother scaped from endless travail-throes,

 But not escaping the malign regard
 Of golden-thronèd Hera,—swaddled lay
  In wraps of saffron hue.
Then hot with wrath the queen of heaven in haste dispatched

Two dragons gray,
Which quickly through the open portals fared
To their bed-chamber wide, and fain had snatched,
Lapped quickly in their coils, away
Both babes.   But he their coming knew,
And raised his head upright, and first began the fray,

Grasping with both his hands the serpents twain
Tight by the neck with force they could not flee,
Till they were choked, and till
Time from their hideous forms the breath of being drove.
Then horrible
Dread like an arrow smote the female train
Who chanced, performing offices of love,
About Alkmena's bed to be ;
For to her feet unrobèd still
She sprang from bed to fend th' assault of brutes so fell.

And fast with brazen weapons thronging ran
The chiefs of Kadmus' folk ; and with them speeding on,
A broadsword brandishing of scabbard bare,
With stricken air
Of bitter anguish,—for his private smart
Goes home to every heart

Alike, but if mishap another man
Befall, we soon take comfort,—came Amphitryon,

And stood amazed with sorrow and delight
Commingled, for he saw th' unnatural
Courage and strength his boy
Possessed, and how the gods the message full of fear
Had falsified.
The prophet then of Zeus supreme in might,
Teiresias his neighbour, truthful seer,
He summoned, who obeyed the call,
And showed him filling him with joy
And all his host what fates the baby should betide ;

How many foul wild beasts by field and flood
He should destroy ; how many evil men,
Walking in crooked way
Of lawless insolence, he should consign to death,
He told ; and how,
On Phlegra's plain when with the giant-brood
The gods should join in battle, felled beneath
The hurling of his javelins then
Full many a foeman bold should lay
His ringlets bright with oil in earth's defilement low :

P

But he himself, in splendid recompense
For wondrous toils endured, uninterruptedly
  In peaceful calm in realms delectable
     For aye should dwell :
  Where blooming Hebe should become his bride,
    And at the feast beside
  Zeus, son of Kronos, he should sit, and thence
Extol that stately home's supreme felicity.

2. To Timodemus of Athens.

As bards who boast themselves the progeny
    Of Homer, when they gin
Recitals of heroic poesy,
    With Zeus are wonted to prelude,
        So this man now
His earnest gains of crowns, that wreathe the brow
    Of them the sacred games that win,
In Nemeän Zeus's song-renownèd wood.

And yet Timonoüs's son is bound,
    If on his father's way,
The pride of mighty Athens, he be found
    Life's path straight-forwardly to tread,
        Oftimes to pluck
The fairest flower of Isthmus' godsent luck ;
    And often shall he win the day

In Pytho's list : as surely as 'tis said

Not distant from the mountain Pleiades
    Orion's star must sail.
And Salamis has many witnesses
    How she a fighting-man can rear :
      For Aias' blow
Hektor on Troas' plain had cause to know.
    And thy pancratic prowess will avail
Thee, Timodemus, higher still to bear.

Time-honoured is Acharnæ's blazonry
    For famous men.   Of all
Foremost in sports the Timodemidæ
    Have always borne away the bell.
      For four times home
From lordly-browed Parnassus they have come
    The heroes of the festival :
And twice four times in good king Pelops' dell

They gained the victor's garland from the men
    Of Corinth, and have here
In Nemeä seven times triumphant been,
    And in Athenian Zeus's games

Won countless times.
To whom for Timodemus raise the rhymes
    Of wassail now, and wish him cheer
And proud return.   Begin your sweet acclaims.

3. To Aristokleides of Aigina.

O venerated Muse, O mother mine,
   I pray thee in the sacred days
      Of Nemeä
Come to the Doric isle Aigina o'er the sea,
      Where strangers aye
   Are welcome.   For beside Asopus' stream
   The youthful choir, who make our games the theme
      Of honied lays,
Await thee, longing sore for that sweet voice of thine.
   Good work is thirsty for its proper meed
   Each in its sort; and songs the rightest seem
To follow him to whom the crown has been decreed
      For bravery.

   Whereof unsparing affluence bestow
    Through craft of mine.   The hymn begin

Acceptable,

O daughter, to the lord of cloud-engirdled heaven ;
And with its swell
My cittern I will join and choral strains,
And th' island's glory pleasurable pains
Shall have, wherein
Dwelt warlike Myrmidons long centuries ago.
Not on their market-place of old renown
Aristokleides brought dishonour's stains
By thy decree ; his strong endurance broke not down,
Though he has striven

The meed of pancratist to win ; and victory
In Nemeä's deep vale can healing bring
For painful blows and labours harassing.
Yet comely though his form, and though his deeds agree
Well with his looks, the son of Aristophanes
Has reached the highest feat he can achieve ;
He will not find it easy work to cleave
The trackless sea beyond the posts of Herakles,

By th' hero-god for famous witnesses
Of that his furthest voyage placed.
When in his strength

He quelled the monsters of the deep, and searchèd through
      The weary length
Of channels mid the shoals, where he might find
Safe passage to the home he left behind,
      And duly traced
The limits of the land.   My spirit, tell me, please,
  For what strange headland settest thou thy sail?
  To Aiakus, I tell thee, and his kind—
For Right supreme enjoins to laud the good—thy tale
      Of song is due.

  "T is not the love of strangers' fame that best
    Befits the singer.   Seek at home
      Thy subject.   There
Thou hast a theme at hand to make thy descant on
      Surpassing fair.
  For kingly Peleus in the ages long
  Agone for bravery rejoiced in song,
      The wondersome
Spearshaft who cut, and took alone without the rest
  Iolkos, and the seaborn Thetis caught
  By violence : and Telamon the strong
At Iolaüs' side to utter ruin brought
      Laomedon ;

And followed him where bows of brass the Amazons
    Handle, nor once did soul-subduing dread
    Check his high spirit. Eminence inbred
Has mighty leverage : but he that only cons
A lesson, blowing hot and cold alternately,
    Ne'er puts his foot with firmness down, but wastes
    Good effort on ten thousand fruitless tastes.
But e'en when staying in the home of Philyre

    Ruddy Achilles in his childhood played
      At deeds heroic ; oft would swing
        In baby hand
His little javelin barbed with steel, and swift as wind
      Would with his brand
    Do murder on the lions 'mid the wold,
    Or slaughter boars. When but a six-year-old
      He 'gan to bring
Their palpitating forms, himself all undismayed,
    To Kronos' Kentaur-son, and aye from this
    Persisted in his triumphs manifold ;
Till bold Athena saw, and huntress Artemis,
      With awestruck mind

    Him kill the deer without or cunning snare

Or aiding hound, for in his feet
　　His strength appeared.
I have a story, told by them of former days,
　　How Cheiron reared
　With deepest counsels in his cavernous
　Home first Iason, next Asklepius,
　　And precepts meet
Taught him, with gentle hand his medicines to prepare.
　There Nereus' noble daughter afterward
　He gave in marriage, and her marvellous
Son tended, all his soul resolved to train and guard
　　In such fit ways

That, carried by the sweep of ocean-winds afar
　To Troas, he might stand the battle-cries
　Of Lykian, Phrygian, Dardan, enemies
Amid the clash of spears, and hand to hand in war
Mix with the spearmen, in his heart determining
　That nevermore to his ancestral home
　Should Helenus' impetuous cousin come,
Memnon the swarthy-skinned, their Ethiopian king.

Thence light that casts far radiance rose upon
　The lineage of Aiakus :

For thine they are,
O Zeus, in blood ; and thine the strife that now in song
    The lads prepare,
  Hymning their country's joy, t' extol ; and well
  Jubilant shouts befit, and music's swell,
    Victorious
Aristokleides, who on their Theärion,
  Pythian Apollo's holy house, bestows
  Illustrious care, and bids their voices tell
The honours of this isle.   Long trial only shows
    The truly strong.

At first among one's fellow boys a boy,
  And then a man with men, the third
    A later stage
With elder folk, one proves how far we men succeed ;
    And long old age
  Makes excellences four, and bids one turn
  One's thoughts to things at hand, nor farther yearn.
    And by my word
This virtue too is his. O friend, I give thee joy,
  And send thee this white milk with honey sprent,
  Where clinging round the bowl thou may'st discern
A draught of song with soft Aiolian pipings blent,

For tardy meed.

Of all the birds that fly the eagle is most fleet
    Of wing, and spies his quarry far away,
    Gives chase, and quickly grasps the gory prey
With ruthless talons; whilst in lowly places meet
The screaming daws.   For thee, my friend, from Nemeä—
    So queenly Klio wills—distinction's beam
    For thy victorious spirit bright doth gleam,
From Epidaurus too, and eke from Megara.

4. To Timasarchus of Aigina.

A FESTIVE bout, when toil is o'er
And judgment done, may best restore
　　Exhausted thews ; and hymns,
The Muses' gifted children, love
Their soothing charms of touch to prove.

　　The ease that weary limbs,
In tepid baths relaxed, obtain
Compares not with the cittern's strain
　　Attuned to words of praise :
For word has longer life than deed,
Whene'er the Graces have decreed
To deeply-musing tongue the meed
　　Of long-protracted days.

Be such my feast-preluding lay
For Kronos' Zeus, and Nemeä,
　　And Timasarchus' feat

Of wrestle.   Let the dwelling-place
Of Aiakus' heroic race,
  This towered island, greet
It well, where law's fair lamp is set
Of help for foreigners.   If yet
  Timokritus thy sire
Could warm him in the fierce sunshine,
His now had been the hand, not mine,
Thy song of triumph to combine
  With his melodious lyre.

Kleonæ's list thy garlands' chain
Began, which Athens twined again,
  Bright city of renown.
In Thebes the seven-portallèd,
Where splendour sepulchres her dead
  Hero Amphitryon,
Her Kadmus' sons delighted wove
With flowers, for Aigina's love,
  Thy locks; for thou wert come,
A friend to friends, the memories
Of ancient hospitalities
Awakening, to Herakles'
  Supremely happy home.

With whom the stalwart Telamon
In days primeval fell upon
 Troy and the Meropes ;
And slew the huge, dread, man of war
Alkyoneus ; but not before   .
 Twelve four-horse carriages,
And twice as many valiant men
Who mounted them or held the rein,
 Beneath his boulders fell.
Witless of battle were the wight,
Who could not understand aright
That he, on whom successes light,
 May light on harm as well.

But custom all I fain would say
Precludes, and hours that will not stay.
 Yet this new moon my heart,
As if by wryneck spell, is bent
The story shortly to present.
 Although, my soul, thou art
Amidst the deep and briny sea
Half-whelmed, resist the treachery :
 Then we in broad daylight
Shall come to land with genial skies,

Superior to our enemies ;
While th' other, envy in his eyes,
  Revolves in gloomy night

His futile earthward thought. To me
What gift imperial Destiny
  Has granted, I know well.
And coming time shall perfect it
As fate decrees. So prythee fit
  To Lydian music's swell,
O sweet my lyre, at once and here,
The theme to fair Oinone dear,
  And Kyprus' sea-beat strand ;
Where Teukros, son of Telamon,
In exile holds a foreign throne ;
While Salamis, by birth his own,
  Obeys her Aias' hand ;

And 'midst the Hospitable Main
His gleaming isle Achilles' reign.
  Fair Thetis Phthia sways ;
And where Epeirus wide is spread,
Beginning from Dodona's head,
  To far Ionia's bays,

In mountain-ridges herds to feed,
The herdsman still reveres the rede
  Of young Neoptolemos :
And proud Iolkos Peleus gave
To Haimon's children, when with glaive
Of foe he sought her, for a slave
  At foot of Pelios,

Ware of the subtle treachery
Akastus' wife Hippolyte
  Had planned ; for Pelias' seed
With curiously-fashioned knife
Laid ambush for the stranger's life.
  But fate by Zeus decreed
Was carried out ; for Cheiron came
And foiled him.   All-subduing flame
  When he had masterèd,
And 'scaped the lion's sharpest claws,
And savage craft, and fearful jaws
With fangs tremendous armed because
  A mortal he would wed

One of the high-enthroned array
Of Nereids, Peleus gat his way ;
  Q

And saw the rounded seat,
Whence they who rule the sky and sea
On him for his posterity
   Their gifts and power great
Bestowed.   To sail is not allowed
Beyond Gadeira's banks of cloud.
   So for the continent
Of Europe trim thy barque again.
At length the glories of the reign
Of Aiakus's sons my strain
   To hymn were vainly bent.

But, as I promised, glad I came
To Isthmus' and Olympia's game
   And Nemeä's, that limbs
Make strong, with ready heraldry
The fame of the Theandridæ
   To blazon in my hymns;
Who from the trial never come
Uncrowned with fruitful honours home.
   And now we hear that these
Thy clansmen, Timasarchus, will
There join the melodies that shrill
Thy triumph.   If thou bid'st me still

To raise for Kallikles,

Thy mother's brother, column new
Than Paros' stone more white of hue ;
　　As brightest lights appear
In smelting gold, so song, the meed
That chronicles his noble deed,
　　Can make a man the peer
Of kings ; and though by Acheron
He dwell, my voice's ringing tone
　　Shall reach him even there.
Because in Corinth's rivalry
Before the thunderous deity
Who wields the trident gaily he
　　The parsley wreath did wear.

And gladsomely thy father's sire,
Old Euphanes, attuned his lyre
　　His praise to chaunt, my boy.
Well—others lived in other days ;
But each man hopes that terms of praise
　　Himself can best employ
For whatso feat himself has seen.
Melesias to laud, I ween,

Of strife would clear the field.
Invincible in speaking, he
To goodly folk benignantly
Behaves, a stubborn enemy
  To them that will not yield.

5. To Pytheas of Aigina.

I AM no sculptor, statued forms to make,
 In idleness impassible
 Aye on the selfsame pedestal
To stand. From our Aigina passage take
By merchantman and skiff, sweet song, and speak
 How Pytheäs, Lampo's strong-limbed-son,
 In Nemeä the crown has won
Of pancratist, ere yet upon his cheek
The summer-tint like tender vine-down shone ;

And graced th' Aiakidæ with fresh renown, —
 The warrior heroes, who from Zeus'
 And Kronos' loins their line deduce
And Nereus' golden maids,—their mother-town
And lands to strangers friendly honouring.
 For whose success upon the brine
 Erst by th' Hellenic Father's shrine

Endeïs' famous sons stood worshipping
With strong king Phokus, raising hands and eyne

To heaven.   Him on the margin of the sea
   The goddess Psamatheä bare.
A deed tremendous dared unrighteously
   I fear to utter ; why the pair
Quitted their glorious isle, and what avenging god
Drove from Oinone men of such high hardihood.
   I stay me.   'T is not always best
   That naked Truth should self-confessed
To all the crowd her fearless forehead show.
'T is wisest oft to hide within the breast
   In silence what we hap to know.

But if to wealth or strength of hand I deem
   My praises due, or iron war,
   Long though the leap they might prepare,
To my knees' agile flight 'twould nothing seem.
The eagles wing their way across the deep :
   And glad the Muses' peerless choir
   Sang them on Pelion, his lyre
Seven-tongued while Phoibos in their midst would sweep
With golden bow, that flashed and leaped like fire

Through strains of many measures.   First they 'gan
   Of Zeus to sing, and Thetis' brow
   So sweetly grave, and Peleus, how
He nigh was trammelled in the crafty plan
 Of Kretheus' dainty child Hippolyte ;
   Who strove her husband to beguile,
   Magnetia's lord, with many a wile,
Piecing together lying tales that he
Akastus' marriage-bed would sully ; while

'T was just the other way.   With burning heart
   And speech she oft solicited
His love : her evil words bred only smart
   And ire : he spurned the girl for dread
Of him who guards the rights of hospitality,
The cloud-assembling Sire, King of immortals.   He
   From heaven perceiving bowed assent ;
   Then quickly to Poseidon went,
For Peleus urging him an Ocean-bride,
A golden-spindled Nereïd, content
   With mortal kinship, to provide.

Oft to the famous Dorian Isthmus he
   From Aigæ's island swiftly speeds,

Where jubilant throngs with vocal reeds
Welcome the god, and show their rivalry
In fearless strength of limb. 'T is Fate decrees
    Their kindred meed of praise to all.
    And there thou in the arms didst fall
Of Victory divine, Euthymenes,
And reap Aigina's choral hymns withal.

And even now thy uncle noble proves
    His kindred folk, who follow in
    His footsteps, Pytheäs, crowns to win.
Him Nemeä and the month Apollo loves,
His country's month, conspired to suit, and he
    All comers of his age at home
    Beat, and in Nisus' lovely coomb.
Well-pleased am I that for the mastery
The whole state strives.   But know thy luck has come

Thanks to Menander, balm for all thy pain.
    The athletes' trainer well may hail
From Athens.   But Themistius if thou fain
    Would'st sing, then shrink not, hoist thy sail
Up to the main-top yard, give thy voice utterance,
And cry aloud how he attained the double chance

To win in Epidaurus' list
In wrestle, and as pancratist ;
And to the porch of Aiakus upbare
Garlands which leaves with blossoms intertwist
Through th' auburn-tressèd Graces' care.

6. To Alkimides of Aigina.

THE race of men
And gods is one ; at one the selfsame mother's breast
We all draw in the breath of life.   But infinite
　　Diversity of powers now divides
　　One from the other : so that we are naught,
　　　　But aye the brazen heaven abides
　　　　　　For them a place of rest.
　　　　　Yet somewhat still in mighty thought
　　　　　　Or form the deathless we
　　　　May near ; although we may not ken
What sort of goal unflinching Destiny
　　　　　　By day or night
　　　　　For us to run for may decree.

　　　　And so but now
Alkimides the proof of consanguinity
Shows for us all to see.   Like fruitful harvest-fields,

That changefully one year produce for men
The yearly food-crop of the plains, and one
   Rest to recruit their strength again ;
     A boyish victor he,
  From Zeus the fortune having won,
    From the belovèd games
  Of Nemeä returns, his brow
With garlands circled, not without his claims
     To whatso yields
   Fame to triumphant wrestlers' names.

He planted every footstep painfully
   Along the ancient track
Praxidamas his father's father made :
For he the first for the Aiakidæ
    The olive wreath
Brought from Alpheius of Olympic victory ;
  And coming five times crowned from Isthmus back,
   And thrice from Nemeä's green glade,
  He saved Sokleides, eldest son
Of Agesimachus, from dark oblivion,
   The worser death.

   For these were three

Who dared to taste of toil, and bearing off its prize
Reached the supremest height of honoured hardihood.
  Nor e'er did heavèn-prospered thews make proud
  Another house with greater store of crowns,
    Won in the valley whither crowd
    With eager, scanning, eyes
   The throngs of all broad Hellas' towns.
    And I do hope my strain
    Of triumph may successfully,
  Like dart from bowstring shot, its aim attain :
     So thither, good
    My muse, I pray, direct again

     Thy glorious gale
Of song. For songs and tales each honourable deed
Of those now passed away accompanied : and these
  Were never scarce among the Bassidæ,
  A race of olden note, that bear their own
    Praise with them, able ceaselessly
    With themes of song to feed,
   Because of mighty works well done,
    Pieria's workmen's tongue.
   For once in Pytho's holy vale
Kallias from the same high lineage sprung,

Who wont to please
Gold-spindled Leto's scions young,

With thongs around his knuckles gained the day,
   And starlike shone at night
In songs the Graces sang by Castaly :
And where in each third year the Amphictyons slay
   The bull beside
Poseidon's grove, the son of Kreon many a day
  The narrow bridge, that bars the angry might
   Of the unresting briny sea,
   Held honoured ; and the lion's wreath
Of parsley Phlious' bare primeval hills beneath
   His tresses tied.

On every side
The paths are open wide for chroniclers that would
This noble isle embellish, since th' Aiakidæ,
  Exceeding merit showing, chances rare
  Have given ; o'er the land and thwart the sea
   Their name was wafted through the air
   Abroad for hardihood ;
   O'erleaping e'en the boundary
   Of Ethiopia's sand,

When Memnon came not in his pride
Back as aforetime to his distant land,
　　Such enmity
　Achilles showed him hand to hand,

　　Down from his car
Leaping to ground, when with his ireful javelin's head
He slew bright Eos' son.　But o'er this wagon-road
　Others have driven teams in olden days.
　Yet carefully I follow in their wake :
　　Though every man, the proverb says,
　　That wave of all will dread
　　The most, whose surges threat to break
　　On his own vessel's bow.
　Still I have glady come from far
Upon a willing back to saddle now
　　My double load
　Of heraldship, proclaiming how

This fifth success, beside the previous score,
　　In contests which we call
Divine, Alkimides has gained of late
For his time-honoured kindred.　Twice before
　　By Zeus's grove

Thou and thy Polytimides of need forswore
　　The flowers of Olympia's festival
　　　Through lots but too precipitate.
　　And swift as dolphin through the sea
Melesias I call, who hands and strength for thee
　　　Like chariot drove.

7. To Sogenes of Ægina.

Oh ! hear me, Eileithuia, thou that sit'st beside
  The three weird sisters deep of thought,
All-potent Hera's most prolific child !
Without thy aid we ne'er had seen the light,
    Nor looked on sable night,
  Nor known thy sister Hebe fair of limb.
Yet not for equal ends are all men brought
    To life, but binding Fates divide
Each one from other.   Yet through thy protection mild
  Has Sogenes, Theärion's noble son,
    The pentathlete's distinction won ;
So are his glories sung in our triumphal hymn.

Because his home is in the isle where song doth dwell ;
    And where the seed of Aiakus
  Love clash of spear, and joy in exercise
  To keep their souls for coming victory.

And he, whose feats may be
By fortune blest, affords the Muses' stream
Matter most sweet.   For prowess marvellous,
    That lacks the song its worth to tell,
Thick darkness shrouds : and we can hold no otherwise
    The mirror up to work well done, save we
        Bright-filleted Mnemosyne
Win to make toil's reward the poet's honoured theme.

    The wise perceive three days before it come
        The signs of windy weather,
Nor run for gain the risk of injury.
        Rich men and poor together
Travel the road whose goal is death ; and we
        Deem not Odysseus bare such doom
As seems from Homer's charming poesy.

Since he by soaring art imparts solemnity
        To fiction, leading us astray
With fables by his lore contrived ; and most
Amongst us men are ever blind of heart.
        For, had there been an art
To know the Truth, then not for armour's sake
Had Aias stout his sword so brightly gray

R

Deep in his bosom thrust ; for he
Except Achilles was the bravest of the host,
   Whom steady-blowing Zephyr's escort bore
     In speedy ships the waters o'er,—
His wife for yellow Menelaüs home to take,—

To Ilus' city. But the wave of Hades flows
     To whelm us all alike, and falls
   On him that waits it and that waits it not.
    But honour springs for them, for whom when dead
      A god prepares the aid
   Of graceful story, who wide-bosomèd
Earth's centre-stone have reached. When Priam's halls
     Neoptolemus had sacked,—the close
Of all the Danaan's long toil,—he saw this spot,
   And lies in Pythian ground ; for sailing home
    Skyros he missed, but happed to roam
To Ephyre at last by devious courses led.

He in Molossia reigned but little while,—
     Though still his seed forever
Have held that honour,—for when nigh he drew
     The altar, to deliver
Troy's first-fruits rare, a fellow of his crew

In quarrel o'er the fleshy spoil
With carving-knife the chief attacked and slew.

And sore the kindly Delphic folk were grieved, although
    He did but pay the debt of fate.
  For need it was that one of kingly birth
  Of Aiakus' descent should aye remain
    Beside the well-built fane
  Of Phoibos, in that oldest close to be
  A resident chief-officer of state,
    The heroes' sacrificial show
To see performed with due respect.   Three words are worth
  Much speaking, since no witness false presides
    O'er Pytho's rites ; no risk betides
Me, when I say that those who come of Zeus and thee,

Aigina, claim renown in right of ancestry
    For shining worth.   But rest is sweet
  In every sort of work ; and honey e'en,
  And Aphrodite's choicest blossoms, breed
    Surfeit in them that feed
  Too long thereon.   By nature each man lives
  A life distinct ; no one of us may meet
    With unalloyed felicity :

That were impossible.   Sharing her gifts between
Us fairly, perfect, lasting, bliss to none
   That I can name has Moira shown :
Still ample share of luck, Theärion, now she gives

   To thee, with daring set on objects high
      Sagacity uniting,
  A guest and stranger I am here to-day,
     Jealous detraction slighting :
  Like one who makes the river water-way
   A friend's dry meads to moisten, I
  Will laud true glory, good men's richest pay.

None of Achaia's men shall blame me, be he nigh
   Though dwelling on Ionia's sea ;
  Here on the public friendship I may lean ;
  And when at home among my countrymen,
     My eye is bright of ken :
  Not passing bounds, out of my path I roll
  All violence. May years oncoming be
   Cheery ; and men shall say if I
To scandal's tattle use my singing to demean.
  O Sogenes, from Euxenus' proud line
   Descended, this quick tongue of mine

Like javelin brazen-cheeked I ne'er beyond the goal

Have sped, I swear it.   Thou from wrestling-feat
  Broughtest thy neck and strength undewed
With moisture, till thy young limbs fell within
The sunshine's scorching reach.   If toil be sore
    Joy follows all the more.
Nay, let me be ; for if perhaps too gay
I cried a little loud, I still am good
  To pay the winner honour meet.
'T is lightsome work to weave the crowns.   The song begin :
  For surely gold and snow-white ivory
  The Muse to-day entwines for thee
With lily-flowers plucked beneath the salt sea spray.

When thou dost mention make at Nemea
    Of Zeus, thou must discreetly
Control the varied tones of those who sing.
    And fit it is that sweetly
Low voices in this plot should praise the king
    Of gods ; for Aiakus, they say,
His mother bore to his high fathering,

Lord of his own fair isle to be, and brother dear

And loving friend, O Herakles,
   To thee.   And if man ever get by man
Advantage, we should say a neighbour's love
      Strong, hearty, true, would prove
Joy to his neighbour worth the world beside.
And if a god would give us gifts like these,
      Oh ! then full fain to dwell anear
Thy temple, who hast quelled the Giants' godless clan,
   With fortune crowned were Sogenes' desire
      In gentle tendance on his sire,
In that rich street where his forefathers lived and died.

For like the pole upon the double-yokèd car
      His home, O blessed hero, lies
   'Twixt thy domains that stretch on either hand.
   Thine is it Hera's husband to persuade,
         And the fierce grey-eyed maid ;
   Nay and thyself to mortals oft canst give
   Aid in embarrassing perplexities.
      Oh ! would that life, with nought to mar
Its happiness, and strength its trials to withstand,
   Thou wouldest weave for them, for youth's glad stage,
      And comfortable, calm, old age !
And that their sons' sons aye may high in honour live

As now, and higher after.   Ne'er did I,—

    I will not make admission,—

Neoptolemus with scurvy words abuse.

    Yet endless repetition

Of praise itself can serve no sort of use :

    As chatter-boxes idly cry

Three times and four, " Korinthus is of Zeus."

8. To Deinis of Aigina.

O ROYAL time of Spring, that heraldest
    Bright Aphrodite's loves divine,
And sitting on the lids of maidens' eyes and boys'
    Wilt one with soft compulsion's gentle hands
      Ennoble, while thy spell destroys
        Or scathes another's breast.
'T is passing sweet to own the power that commands
    In every case love's better joys,
Nor wander from the path when Fortune is benign.

  'T was thus the shepherds of the gifts conferred
    By her of Kyprus o'er the bed
Of Zeus and of Aigina watched ; and thence arose
    A son, Oinone's king, alike the best
      In counsel calm and heavy blows.
        And many prayers were heard
Of men that they might see him : for uncalled, unpressed.

The bravest of the heroes chose,
Who dwelt around, by him as chieftain to be led ;

They who in rocky Athens kept her host
    In discipline, and Pelops' seed,
  Lords of the Spartan land.   In suppliance
I clasp the venerated knees of Aiakus
  For this dear isle and these her habitants,
    Bearing my Lydian chaplet, wrought
      With many a curious
  Device of thrilling song and sounding reed,
  For Deinis' double course from Nemeä brought
  To make his father Meges glorious.
For weal with heaven begot aye stays by men the most.

With wealth erewhile this loaded Kinyras
    In sea-girt Kyprus. Now I stand
Tiptoe afoot, and draw my breath before I speak.
  For much has oft been told and many-wise :
    Yet great the peril if one seek
      And find new truth, alas !
For proof to lay it on the touchstone. Dainty prize
    Are tales to Envy's tongue, the weak
That ne'er assaults, but stalks the noblest in the land.

Envy devoured the son of Telamon ;
    For this upon his sword he died :
For in the dismal strife oblivion is the meed
    Of one not quick of speech but bold of heart ;
        And highest honours are decreed
            To falsehood's shifty tone.
For Greeks with votes clandestine took Odysseus' part ;
    And spoiled of th' arms of gold, his right indeed,
Aias was left alone to combat suicide.

Yet not alike the wounds in battle free
    They dealt hot-blooded on the foe,
        Some round Achilles' body scarcely cold,
Some in the other toils of those disastrous days,
    'Neath the protecting lance.   But e'en of old
        Hateful Deception had her hour ;
            Who travels in the ways
    Where Flattery and Guile are wont to go,
Wily of mind, an ill of baleful power,
    That presses hard on brilliancy, to raise
The rotten fame of one meet for obscurity.

Be ne'er such habit mine, O father Zeus ;
    To simple paths of life let me

Hold fast, that dying I may leave my sons a fame
　　Unsmirched by evil rumour.　Some men pray
　　　For gold, and others fain would claim
　　　　Unbounded lands to use;
But I desire in earth my limbs to hide away
　　　In favour with my fellows, blame
Casting on all things foul, and lauding bravery.

For merit, as a tree fed by gray dews
　　Shoots up toward the moistened air,
Grows aye more perfect, by the just of men and wise
　　Being exalted.　Great and manifold
　　　Needs of a friendly hand arise :
　　　　And though its highest use
Be seen in trouble, joy is eager to behold
　　　Proof of itself before its eyes.
Meges my friend, to bid thy soul again repair

To earth is past my strength ; and wishes vain
　　　Have empty ending.　But I can
　　Build for thy house and the Chariadæ
A mighty monument of song, to celebrate
　　Two lucky pairs of feet.　And joyfully
　　　I vaunt me as befits the deed :

For song has magic great
To kill the pain of toil for toiling man.
And festal hymns, the conqueror's best meed,
Were known to singers of remotest date ;
Before Adrastus fought, or Kadmus' kin were slain.

9. To Chromius of Etna.

COME, Muses ; from Apollo's home
In Sikyon we'll lead the brawls
To new-built Etna till we come,
And enter Chromius' happy halls ;
Where yielding gates' fly open wide
Before his guests' triumphant tide.
But words with sweetest minstrelsy
Combine ; for when his conquering
Chariot he mounts, he claims that we
A song should to the Mother sing,
And to her children twain, who keep
Together watch o'er Pytho's lofty steep.

An ancient proverb serves to bid
That honest work, when fairly done,
Should never be in silence hid

Beneath the ground. Th' exultant tone
Of song divine may fittest suit
High deeds : and we the sounding lute
And fife will rouse to hymn the prime
Of games, where steeds of famous blood
Contend, which in the olden time
Adrastus by Asopus' flood
Stablished for Phoibos' sake : and we
Will deck with honours for their memory

The hero who was monarch then ;
And there in novel festival,
Where hollow cars and valiant men
As rivals strove, displayed to all
His city's glory. For he fled,
Through bold Amphiaraüs' dread,
To 'scape sedition murderous
From Argos and his father's home ;
Since there the sons of Talaüs
Bare rule no longer, overcome
By faction : for the stronger hand
Puts down the early usage of a land.

But Eriphyle, fatal wife,

When to Oikleus' son they gave,
For surety leal of ended strife,
They grew the greatest 'mong the brave
Yellow-haired Danaans : so they
In those old days their host's array
To Thebes the seven-gated led
Without one favourable sign
From flight of birds ; nor overhead
Did Zeus, who makes the lightning shine,
Urge them from home in eager pride ;
But bade them from the journey turn aside.

So swift to ruin sure and clear
Sped that ill-omened army's ranks,
With brazen arms and splendid gear
Of steeds.   But on Ismenus' banks,—
Sweet hopes of home-returning dead
And gone,—they with their bodies fed
The thick white smoke.   For seven pyres
Feasted on young limbs fresh and brave :
But Zeus, who wields th' eternal fires,
With thunderbolt resistless clave
Deep-bosomed Earth, and hid in death
Amphiaraüs and his steeds beneath,

Ere Periklymenus's spear
Had struck him in the back, and made
His warrior's soul ashamed : for fear,—
When gods conspire to make afraid,—
Puts even sons of gods to flight.
O son of Kronos, if it might
So be, I fain would long delay
This bold but sore arbitrament,
Where life and death hang on the fray,
With yon Phoinikian armament ;
And pray thee grant that orderly
The lot of Etna's children long may be.

Nay I would rather they should choose
In civic triumphs their success.
For men there are there, father Zeus,
Who love the steed, and souls possess
Superior to gain, although
Untrusty sound my words, I know.
For unawares is Modesty
Despoiled by love of gain, though fraught
With glory : but hadst thou been by
When foot, and horse, and navies, fought,
Chromius' shield-bearer, thine had been

Throughout the risk of battle's piercing din

    To judge in stress of fight how well
    That selfsame goddess Modesty
    Nerved his brave spirit to repel
    The War-god's havoc. Few there be
    With limbs and soul and wit to know
    To turn upon the marshalled foe
    That dreadful cloud, when big with blood
    About their feet and o'er their head
    It gathers. By Scamander's flood
    For Hektor glory's flower is said
    Once to have bloomed ; and so beside
The beetling cliffs that hem Helorus' tide,

    Hard by the well-known ford that bears
    Areä's name, this light has shone,
    In early prime of manhood's years,
    Upon Agesidamus' son.
    And many a tale have I to tell
    Of struggles where he bore him well,
    Some on the dusty plain, and some
    On yonder sea, its neighbour bright.
    And out of toils is wont to come,

When young men toil with purpose right,
Calm in old age.　Then let him wot
What wondrous bliss the gods have made his lot.

For if to wealth's abundant store
Be joined illustrious repute,
A mortal man may strive no more
On other heights to plant his foot.
But friends at banquet met delight
In quiet ; and triumphant might,
Though fresh its youthful vigour be,
Will gather strength from gentle song ;
And when the bowl is flowing free
Unwonted courage fires the tongue.
Then straight let some one mix for me
This welcome harbinger of revelry.

The headstrong offspring of the vine
Let them in silver goblets pour ;
Which late, on Chromius' board to shine,
From Sikyon's god-haunted shore
His matchless mares have gained and sent,
With Phoibos' well-won chaplets blent.
O father Zeus, to thee I pray,

Grant me the Graces' aid to sing
This worthy deed ; and let my lay,
His newest triumph dowering
With honour, many lays excel,
Striking the Muses' mark with aim invincible !

10. To Theaius of Argos.

THE town of Danaüs
With fifty daughters each on splendid throne,
Argos, the worthy home of Hera's godship sing,
   Ye Graces; for she shines with excellence
     Of hardy deeds in days far hence.
       'T were tedious
What Perseus with Medusa's Gorgon-head
Performed to tell; or how in Egypt Epaphus
   Established cities fair past numbering;
Nor when she kept her sword, in purpose all alone,
Safe in its sheath was Hypermnestra's soul misled.

   And once the yellow-tressed
  Gray-eyed Athena made a god divine
Of Diomedes; once, smit by the bolt of Zeus,
   The Theban soil Oïkleus' prophet-son,
     War's very storm-cloud, closed upon:

And still she best
Is famed for fair-haired women.   Zeus of old
Seeking Alkmena's arms and Danaë's confessed
    This ancient saying true.   She too the use
Gave to Adrastus' son and Lynkeus to combine
Perfect uprightness with ripe wisdom manifold,

And nursed the courage of Amphitryon.
        Nay and the mightiest
    In bliss to his affinity
        Came down, for when
With brazen weapons the Teleboæ
He slew, the king of gods his semblance deigned to don,
        And to his chamber pressed,
    Bearing the fearless seed of Herakles ;
        Whose matchless bride,
        Fairest of goddesses,
    Hebe, Olympus treads beside
The Mother who fulfils the vows of men.

        Too poor my tongue to tell
    All the good things that fate has made the share
Of Argos' wide domains : and envious folk are hard
    To meet.   But still thy well-strung lyre awake,

Bid her of wrestling-matches take
Good heed and well.
For lo ! to Hera's solemn sacrifice
The brazen contest bids the eager people swell,
To see each winner get his own reward :
And Oulias's son Theaius winning there
Has patient labour drowned in sweet oblivion twice.

He in the days gone by
All Hellas' host at Pytho o'erthrew ;
And coming companied by fortune gained the crown
At Isthmus and at Nemeä, to yield
The Muses an unfurrowed field ;
Three times he won
By the sea's gates, and on the sacred plain
Thrice by Adrastus' laws in peerless might he shone.
O father Zeus, his tongue will not make known
His soul's desires ; but all result to thee is due :
No faint-heart he that prays so boldly grace to gain.

Known to Theaius and to all, who e'er
Strive for the chiefest prize
Of th' highest games, I tell my tale :
How over all

The Pisan rites of Herakles prevail :
But twice Theaius' feats to dithyrambic air
    At Athens' mysteries
Sweet voices have proclaimed in revel-song ;
      And once in clay
    Fire-hardened to the strong
    People of Hera came the gray
Old olive's fruit in jars pictorial.

    Thick on thy mother's race
Of wide renown the contests' honours fall,
Theaius, granted by the Graces and the twin
    Tyndaridæ.   But I would never hide,
      Were I to Thrasyklus allied,—
        As is thy case,—
    And Antias, the radiance of my eyes
From Argos' folk.   For count how many triumphs grace
Proitus' horse-breeding city.   To begin
Four times betwixt her bays at Corinth's festival,
And from Kleonæ's men four times they took the prize ;

    Then home from Sikyon
Enriched with silver wine-cups they returned ;
And from Pellene came with cloaks upon their backs

Of softest wool; but all their countless plate
And bronzes to enumerate
Would lay upon
Me more than I can do.   A longer space
Of leisure time 't would need to tell them one by one,
At Kleitor, Tegeä, in the mountain-tracks
Of rough Achaia's towns, or on Lykaius earned
Nigh Zeus's fane by strength of hand or speed of pace.

Since Kastor erst and Polydeukes came
Twin boys petitioning
Old guestship's rights from Pamphaës,
We marvel not
To find inbred in them the qualities
Of right good wrestlers.   For the fate of every game
Is in the ordering
Of ample Sparta's lords, with Herakles'
And Hermes' aid.
And just men's honour these
Their special care have always made :
Yea faithful is the race by gods begot.

And interchanging still
Alternate days, they live for one beside

Their loving father Zeus, and lie the next beneath
   Earth's bowels in the vales of Therapne,
      Filling an equal destiny.
         This lot the will
Of Polydeukes chose, rather than dwell
Wholly a god for aye upon Olympus' hill,
   When Kastor had in combat met his death;
With javelin-point of bronze when Idas smote his side,
While for his missing kine his wrath was terrible.

     Far from Taÿgetus,
  As on an oaken bole the brothers sate,
Lynkeus upon his watch espied them; for his sight
   The sharpest was that ever earthly man
    Was gifted with: then straight they ran
      Impetuous
With nimble feet, and schemed a mighty doom
To bring about.   But in one end calamitous
  The sons of Aphareus were through the might
Of Zeus involved: for Leda's son precipitate
Came in pursuit; and they against their father's tomb

   Stood up to meet him.   There a polished stone,
     The head-piece of the grave,

Grasping, at Polydeukes' breast
> They hurled it: yet
They crushed him not, nor made him in the least
Give back; but rushing on through Lynkeus' mid-rib bone
> His spear's quick point he drave.
And Zeus his smoking bolt on Idas' head
> Cast, fraught with flame:
> And both lay scorched and dead
> Unholpen. 'T is a losing game
For man against a stronger power to fret.

> Then swiftly back again
To his strong brother Tyndareus's son
Hasted, and found him not yet dead, but every breath
> Laboured and rough; then dropped hot tears beside
> His body, and with groanings cried
> Aloud, " From pain,
O father son of Kronos, what shall be
Deliverance? For me, great Sovereign, ordain
> That with my brother I partake his death.
Honour from one bereft of those he loves is gone;
And few of men are true in dire extremity

> Of toil to take their share."

This was his plaint ; and Zeus before him came,
And spake these words : " Thou art my son ; but afterward
  Her hero-husband in thy mother's bed
    Of mortal seed thy brother bred.
       But come howe'er,
  I give thee choice of two alternatives.
If thou thyself alone wouldst on Olympus care,
  Escaping death and eld that men regard
With hate, to dwell with me for evermore the same,
Where my Athena, where black-speared Ares lives,

  This destiny is thine : but if thou wilt
    Still for thy brother's sake
   Contend, and all thy lot with him
     To share dost ask,
  Then shalt thou half thy days dwell in the dim
Regions beneath the earth, and half among the gilt
    Abodes of heaven."   Thus spake
  The king of gods to Polydeukes.   He
     No doubtful choice
    Expressed.   Then speedily
   'Gan Zeus the eyes and then the voice
  To loose of Kastor of the brazen casque.

11. To Aristagoras of Tenedos.

DAUGHTER of Rheä whose it is to sway
  The civic hearth-stone, sister of most high
Zeus and his partner Hera, Hestia,
  Our Aristagoras to thy retreat
    With these his friends make welcome nigh
Thy shining sceptre, since by this thy worship they
Keep Tenedos their home upright upon her feet;

  Much with libations glorifying thee
  As first of gods, and much with burning fat:
While lyre and song unite their melody,
  And with perpetual feasts we celebrate
    Zeus who protects the stranger; that
So Aristagoras may, rich in dignity,
His twelvemonth's task fulfil with heart unharmed by fate.

  And I congratulate

His sire Arkesilas on such a son,
Of form so fair and fearlessness innate.
But if a man possessed of wealth excel
     The comeliness
Of other men, and strength have shown
As winner in the games, let him remember well
     He still must don
    On mortal limbs the festal gown,
And will at last have nought but earth for dress.

Yet should he have the favourable word
Of fellow-townsmen ; and 't is right that we
With honied hymns should make his praises heard,
And paint his virtues.   By the folk around
    For wrestle, and the mastery
Of pancratist, with wreaths on conquerors conferred
He and his famous clan have sixteen times been crowned.

His parents' hesitating hope and fear
Their mighty son withheld, when fain to try
At Pytho and Olympia ; and I swear
I throughly am convinced that, had he come
    To thy clear waters, Castaly,
Or Kronos' shady hill, in prowess more than peer

Of rival combatants he thence had hied him home,

     The solemn revelry
Of the quinquennial feast of Herakles
First having led, with darkling greenery
Of olive round his tresses tied.   But one
     Of mortal mould
  His empty-headed pride has thrown
Out of good fortune ; one a soul, that dares not run
    The risk it sees,
  Drags backward from success his own,
O'ercome with fright of being overbold.

   'T were easy work his ancient ancestry
To piece from Sparta and Peisandros' blood ;
For with Orestes from Amyklæ he
A host of brazen-armed Aiolians led
    Hither.   And by Ismenus' flood
From Melanippus' loins his mother's family
Their blended worth derive. And excellence inbred

   Of old, although for generations strange,
  Recovers strength again. The swarthy field
  Gives not its yearly crop without a change ;

Nor do the trees the fragrance of their bloom
    Always with equal richness yield
Through all the circling years' interminable range,
But vary evermore. So mortal folk does Doom

    Conduct. There comes nowhence
  Sure sign from Zeus to men : but ne'ertheless
  We tread the paths of proud self-confidence,
  Our hearts on much performance bent ; for aye
    With hopes that know
  No shame our limbs are girt around ;
And forethought's golden streams lie very far away.
    For greediness
  Of gain a limit must be found ;
  But mad loves unattained work keener woe.

FRAGMENTS.

T

I. Of Epinikia or Songs of Triumph.

I.

FAMOUS is Aiakus in tale, and great
  Aigina's naval fame :
But when the Dorian army, sped by fate
Divine, of Hyllus and Aigimius came,
  They took it for themselves ; but still
  Subject to ancient rule they dwell ;
No law of gods or men in stubborn will
O'erriding : but their neighbours they excel,
As dolphins other fishes in the sea ;
  And prudent stewards are
  Of all the Muses fare,
And where the wrestlers strive for mastery.

II.

Take from Taÿgetus Lakonias' hound,

If thou wouldst have the wisest of her race

Wild beasts to chase.

And Skyros' goats are found

The best above the milking-pail to stand.

From Argos get thy panoply

Of arms ; thy war-car from the land

Of Thebes ; but if thou wouldst a fancy carriage see,

That thou must seek in fruitful Sicily.

III.

And 't is a fitting meed

That men of worth in choicest song should be

Extolled ; for in no other wise

Can words lay hold of immortality

Of honour ; and a noble deed

Forgotten, dies.

2. Of Threnoi, or Dirges.

I.

FOR them the sun in all his strength below
    Shines, when with us 't is night :
  And meads with crimson roses' glow
    Before their town are dight ;
    And in the shade the trees
Bend down with frankincense and golden fruit.
    And there some please
Themselves with feats of horseback exercise,
And some with draughts, and others with the lute.
  And every sort of happiness
    Blooms in luxuriance there :
    Whilst a sweet odour lies
  For aye above that land so fair
From them that mingle victims numberless
    With fire, whose radiance shines

Afar, upon the gods' well-tended shrines.

II.

By blessèd destiny
Each one of us an end attains
Where labour gets release.
And though with all
The body at the bidding needs must be
Of overpowering death, there yet remains
Life's spirit still alive.
For this alone
Is from the gods: but whilst the limbs can strive
It sleeps; yet oft in dreams has shown
To men asleep at ease
The judgment soon to fall
Of pleasant or of sad futurity.

III.

Souls of the impious
In killing pains, excluded from the sky,
Flit restless over earth's broad face,
With gyves about their limbs

Of ills they cannot fly :
But pious souls in heaven their dwelling-place
Sing God Almighty's praise in tuneful hymns.

IV.

For some, from whom Persephone
Accepts atonement for an ancient wrong,
  Back to the sun above
 In the ninth year their souls she gives.
  From these arise
Great kings of matchless might and noble lives,
 And sages eminently wise.
  And men thereafter love
To call them holy heroes through the long
 Remainder of the years to be.

3. Of Dithyramboi, or Hymns in honour of Dionysus

I.

COME hither to the dance,
Olympian gods, and send us glorious Grace,
Ye who frequent
The city's crowded centre, where the scent
Of incense hangs about the holy walls
Of Athens, and her famous market-place
Gorgeous with ornament.
Accept our out-poured offering
Of wreaths of violets fresh-plucked in spring :
And look on me as, by the will of Zeus
I for the second time advance
To th' ivy-girdled god with noble song,
Whom mortal language calls
Bromius, the Mighty Shouter. Here I came
To hymn the offspring of a sire most high

And a Kadmeian dame.
In Argive Nemeä the sprig of palm
'Scapes not the prophet's eye,
Soon as the Season's chamber-doors are loose,
And nectar-laden plants perceive the scent
Of Spring's fresh balm.
Then tufts of violets are spread
Over the ground in loveliness divine,
And roses in our locks we twine.
Sound therefore, choric throng,
With flutes and vocal melody,
Sound, loudly sound, the praise of Semele,
Who wears the twisted fillet round her head.

II.

O Athens, glorious town,
Resplendent, circled with thy crown
Of violets and song,
Thou only strong
Bulwark of Hellas, city marvellous * * *

III.

* * * to thee,
    Great Mother Kybele,
The cymbals as they whirl the rites begin,
And clashing castanets increase the din,
    And through the air
The blazing yellow pine-wood torches flare.

4. Of Prosodia or Processional Hymns.

I.

ALL hail! thou god-built daughter of the sea,
  Offshoot of earth
To glossy-tressèd Leto's children twain most dear,
 This wide-spread world's unmoving progeny,
   Whom mortals Delos' isle,
 But blessed gods upon Olympus style
  Our darkling earth's conspicuous star,
  * * * * *
 For formerly by winds and buffets wild
 Of many a tempest she was borne about :
   But soon as Koius' child
  Came to her in the throes of birth,
    Four columns stout
 On adamantine bases 'gan uprear
Themselves from Earth's deep roots that stretch afar

Unseen, and on their capitals they bare
The rock ; and there
After her pains 't was hers her happy babes to see.

II.

What can inspire
The bard with sweeter zest,
Or when he takes or lays aside his lyre,
Than hymning Leto of the ample vest,
And them that speed
The fleetness of the steed?

III.

Nay by Olympian Zeus I thee entreat,
O golden Pytho, famed for prophecy,
With Aphrodite to thy sacred seat
And with the Graces, welcome me
The mouthpiece of Pieria's minstrelsy !

5. Of Skolia, or Wassail-songs.

I.

YE damsels of the hospitable kind,
　　Who on Persuasion wait
In wealthy Corinth, who to honour her
Oft burn the yellow tears of paly trees
　　Of frankincense, and fly in mind
To bow before the Mother-queen of Love,
　　The heavenly Aphrodite ; she
　　　　Has granted ye,
O children, her indulgence from above,
　　Your prime's soft fruit
To gather in the beds of pleasant ease.
　　And all is fair when man with fate
　　　　Contends.　But what of me,
I wonder, will the lords of Isthmus say,
So sweet beginning of a roundelay

Who make to suit
Women of questionable character?
Nay, we have learned with touchstone pure to prove
   The qualities of gold   *
     *   *   *   *

Then come, O queen of Kyprus, to thine house :
  For Xenophon has hither led
  To this thy grove a hundred head
Of wild girls in his joy at granted vows.

II.

'T is meet, my soul, of love to pluck the fruits,
    Whilst prime of manhood suits ;
But whoso looks upon the sparkling rays
   Of young Throxenus's eyes,
And tosses not on billows of desire ;
     O'er a cold fire
His gloomy heart of adamant was wrought,

Or iron : or by some quick glance awry
    Of Aphrodite's eye
He has been scorned, and spends laborious days
 . For riches, or in soul he tries

With woman's courage still his road to keep
　　Albeit steep.
But I, like wax of honey-bees, am brought

To dwining as one stung, when face to face
　　　I look upon
　　The smooth fresh limbs of budding youth.
　　　And now in sooth
In Tenedos Persuasiveness and Grace
　　Dwell in Agesilas's son.

III.

　　O Thrasyboulus, friend,
This vehicle of dulcet songs I send
　　　For supper's end.
　　And may they welcome be
　　To them that quaff with thee
The fruit of Dionysus' husbandry,
And motive of Athenian revelry

6. Of a Hymn to the Sun in Eclipse.

BEAM of the Sun that see'st all things that are,
Thou parent of the quickness of mine eyes,
    Supremest star,
    Wherefore withdrawn by day
Hast thou man's soaring powers helpless made,
  And barred the travel of the wise?
  For hurrying along the way
    Of darkness, thou
Art driving some new course untried before.
  Nay but by Zeus I thee implore,
    Turn now thy steeds divine,
And this the universal prodigy,
  To unalloyed prosperity
For Thebes. But if thou bringest us a sign
Of some fresh war, or crops in ruin laid,
  Or an excessive fall of snow,
    Or fatal civil war,

Or ocean's overflow
O'er the dry land, or fields in ice-grip bound,
Or summer of south winds juicy with rain
   Tempestuous; or if thou now
   Wilt drown the earth, and make again
A brand-new race of men to till the ground;
   Then with the wailing train
I too will suffer, but will not complain.

7. Of Sundry Odes.

I.

SHALL we Ismenus praise,
Or golden-spindled Melia,
Or Kadmus, or the holy brood
Born of the Sown, or Thebe's purple snood,
Or Herakles' unflinching might,
Or Dionysus' mirth-begetting rite,
Or bridal of whitearmed Harmonia?

   *   *   *   *   *

In the primeval days
Was heavenly Themis sage as fair
With steeds of gold from Ocean's bed
By the three Fates to th' holy ladder led,
'Mid bright Olympus' paths to be
Preserving Zeus's first-wed wife, and she
The fruitful, true, gold-snooded Seasons bare.

II.

What hopest thou to find in wisdom's lore,
Wherein one man a little may excel
   His fellow ? It can never be
   That mind of mortal should explore
The counsels of the gods on high that dwell
   In immortality.
   And him a mortal mother bore.

III.

   To them that try it not
War is a pleasant thing, but one, whose lot
Has been to try it, shudders when he sees
   Approaching enemies.

IV.

   When god makes plain
The start for each event, the path is straight
   The palm of worthiness to gain,
And better endings on performance wait.

V.

If ever citizen
Guide his community
To rest and quietness,
Then let him seek the beaming light to find
Of self-sufficing unobtrusiveness;
Revengeful faction ousting from his mind;
Whose gifts are penury,
Who ever proves a cruel nurse to men.

VI.

'T is possible to God from darkest night
To bid arise the undefilèd day
Of sunshine; or when noon is full and bright
Its sheen in murk of clouds to hide away.

VII.

O Truth, great queen, thou fount and origin
Of virtue's might,
Snare not, I pray, my plighted promise in
The liar's evil plight.

VIII.

When from the breasts of men
Anxiety with all her toil departs ;
   And on a sea
Of over-golden riches we
   Swim all alike
For a deceitful shore.
He that was poor before has plenty then,
   And rich men multiply their store ;
   While home upon their hearts
Shafts from the bow of Dionysus strike.

IX.

The horse is best for driving,
   The ox befits the plough,
The dolphin quickly diving
   Goes by the galley's prow ;
But if thou wouldst behind thee
   Bear homeward, safe and sound,
The slain wild boar, then find thee
   The brave, enduring, hound.

X.

One glories in the honours of the course,
The crowns that wreathe the whirlwind-footed horse;
  Some love a life that's led
    In gilded bed;
And some in safety where the salt seas toss
Delight in galley swift the brine to cross.

XI.

Stirred from his rest he roamed o'er land and sea,
On mighty mountain out-looks rested he,
And searched the forest-nooks and clefts in misery.

XII.

  What must I do to be
Thy friend, O mighty Thunderer, dread son
  Of Kronos, what to make me one
  Of those the Muses reckon dear,
The constant favourite of kindly cheer?
  This, only this, I ask of thee.

XIII.

Then forth from all the flocks there bubbled out,
Like purest water from the fountain-head,
Fresh milk ; and they to fill their pitchers sped,
And ne'er a leathern jug nor pot of stone
  In all the dwellings thereabout
    Kept holiday ;
  But bowls of wood, and jars of clay
  Were filled to brimming every one.

XIV.

Show not to strangers whatso harm betide
  Us ; this to thee I say.
  If fair success and pleasant cheer
  Be thine, in public straight appear,
  That all the folk thy luck may hear.
But if God send misfortune in thy way,
'T is best a man should this in darkness hide.

www.ingramcontent.com/pod-product-compliance
Lightning Source LLC
Chambersburg PA
CBHW020953030726
47496CB00005B/1494